Praise for

My Documents

"In this excellent collection, as in all his work, memory is put under a microscope, and the division between author and characters is never certain. . . . Zambra's stories are always—or always allege to be—acts of remembrance, and the care he takes to let his readers know that suggests something distinctive about his method."
—*The Guardian*

"[These stories] are discrete tales that blend together with an impressive fluidity. Zambra's characters, who have many of the same personal habits (smoking, listening to '80s pop) and secret predilections (writing poetry, experimenting sexually), seem part of a big, fragmented novel. . . . The author's charming cast examines religion, soccer, relationships, and the lure of solitude—all from a distinctly Chilean perspective. But the view is also a youthful one, neatly capturing the puzzling process of trying to figure out who you really are."
—*Entertainment Weekly*

"Zambra is a direct literary descendant of his older, late compatriot Bolaño. He serves us black, urgent humor with a quotidian casualness, a deceptive simplicity. . . . The single thread of belief for some of Zambra's protagonists is literature itself and its ability, through plain, naked language, to present life as it is felt and lived. . . . Zambra's work possesses a historical sadness that has no time for the gloss of nostalgia. It's a literature that believes in itself, even when it's mired in despair."
—*Bookforum*

"Touching."
—*The Wall Street Journal*

"Zambra finds beauty in the anguish, meaning in the mundane, and an elemental spark of fire in even the flintiest parts of our human hearts."
—*The Denver Post*

"Zambra's latest is also his best. . . . A truly beautiful book."
—Daniel Alarcón, author of *At Night We Walk in Circles*

"Zambra has enormous skill for conveying lush emotional landscapes with stripped and distant language." —Electric Literature

"Extraordinary . . . These pages are animated by candid, familiar voices in whose recollections we become gently imbricated."
—*Words Without Borders*

"Zambra's stories convey with striking honesty what it's like to be Chilean today." —*Publishers Weekly* (starred review)

"Winningly arch and unusual takes on common household predicaments." —*Kirkus Reviews*

"Zambra continues to portray in his writing the depth of feeling that humans bring forth in each other. . . . Zambra's impeccable style and knowledge of humanity are central to [*My Documents*]."
—*Booklist*

PENGUIN BOOKS

MY DOCUMENTS

Alejandro Zambra is the author of ten books, including *Chilean Poet*, *Multiple Choice*, *Bonsai*, *The Private Lives of Trees*, and *Ways of Going Home*. A recipient of a Cullman Center fellowship from the New York Public Library, he has won the English PEN Award and the PEN/O. Henry Award and was a finalist for the Frank O'Connor International Short Story Award. His work has been published in *The New Yorker*, *The New York Times Magazine*, *The Paris Review*, *Granta*, *McSweeney's*, and *Harper's Magazine*, among other publications. He lives in Mexico City.

Megan McDowell (translator) is the recipient of a 2020 Award in Literature from the American Academy of Arts and Letters. Her translations have won the National Book Award, the English PEN Award, and the PEN/O. Henry Award, among other honors, and have been nominated four times for the International Booker Prize.

My
Documents

Alejandro Zambra

TRANSLATED BY
Megan McDowell

PENGUIN BOOKS

PENGUIN BOOKS
An imprint of Penguin Random House LLC
penguinrandomhouse.com

First published in the United States of America by McSweeney's 2015
This edition, with five new stories, published by Penguin Books 2024

Some of these translated works originally appeared, in different form, in *BOMB
Magazine, Harper's Magazine, McSweeney's Quarterly Concern, The New Yorker,
The Paris Review, Tin House, Vice, Words Without Borders,* and *The Yale Review.*

LIBRARY OF CONGRESS CATALOGING-IN-PUBLICATION DATA
Names: Zambra, Alejandro, 1975– author. | McDowell, Megan, translator.
Title: My documents / Alejandro Zambra ; translated by Megan McDowell.
Other titles: Mis documentos. English
Description: [New York] : Penguin Books, 2024. | "Originally published in Spanish
as Mis documentos by Editorial Anagrama, Barcelona"
Identifiers: LCCN 2023004124 (print) | LCCN 2023004125 (ebook) |
ISBN 9780143136521 (paperback) | ISBN 9780525508045 (ebook)
Subjects: LCSH: Zambra, Alejandro, 1975- —Translations into English. |
LCGFT: Short stories.
Classification: LCC PQ8098.36.A43 M913 2023 (print) |
LCC PQ8098.36.A43 (ebook) | DDC 863/.64—dc23/eng/20230127
LC record available at https://lccn.loc.gov/2023004124
LC ebook record available at https://lccn.loc.gov/2023004125

Printed in the United States of America
1st Printing

Set in Adobe Caslon Pro

For Josefina Gutiérrez Parra

Contents

Part 4

Part 5

Translator's Note

I am perhaps the most avid and completist reader of Alejandro Zambra out there. I have translated all of his books, which means I've read them many times in both Spanish and my own English. I've had the pleasure of talking at length with Alejandro about the thinking and experiences that have informed his work. And even so, whenever I return to a particular work after some time away, I discover something new. I think this must have to do with the space he leaves in a text for the reader, which makes it so that whatever or whoever I am when I read, I take something different from it, I fit differently into that space.

It's been ten years since Zambra and I worked together on *My Documents*. It was the third book of his I had translated, and his first short story collection. I was at the beginning of my career, still learning (I am, of course, *still* learning). I remember feeling that Alejandro's book of short stories, ironically, gave him more room to spread out than his novels. Unlike his first two books, this one stretched to a comparatively whopping 272 pages and unfurled a range of voices that weren't always the carefully pruned ones of *Bonsai*, *The Private Lives of Trees*, and *Ways of Going Home*. There is the expansive voice of "Thank You," where we first see the branching, run-on voice that later returns in parts of *Chilean Poet*. There are melancholic voices—I remember tears in my eyes every time I got to the end of "Camilo," maybe thinking this time the story wouldn't end *that* way. There are, especially, inquisitive voices—Zambra is constantly questioning assumptions, and seems to love and distrust the act of writing in equal measure.

Zambra's self-examination through fiction, one might say, reached a critical point in *My Documents*. The book includes many of the themes he returns to repeatedly in his work: the experience of growing up in dictatorship; technology, seemingly monolithic and soon obsolete; the uncertain middle class; and, of course, literature, which is to say fiction, which is to say a prevailing concern with truth. And now, upon returning to this book that is a touchstone in my own literary life, I see even more clearly that *My Documents* is part of a longer, overarching exploration that runs throughout Zambra's work, one that has to do with an intense questioning of ideas of legitimacy and authority, two words that are not synonyms but are intimately bound up with each other. This line of interrogation offers a point of entry into nearly all of his books and stories, and for *My Documents* in particular, it could be useful to examine the stories through these lenses in many respects, but especially, I believe, with regard to his treatment and questioning of masculine roles.

I have long been aware of the position of ambiguity or uncertainty from which Zambra approaches his stories and his characters, both male and female, which counterintuitively manifests in an insistence on specificity, a refusal to lean on cliché. Over the course of his career, he has been putting the microscope to masculinity using a variety of lenses, from the political to the domestic and familial. Especially beginning with *The Private Lives of Trees*, which focused on a male protagonist whom we see solely in the interior, domestic space in the role of caregiver; continuing with *Ways of Going Home*, in which the male narrator's authorial voice is called into question by both the "fictional" Claudia and the "real" Eme; and continuing through to *Chilean Poet* and the newly published *Literatura infantil*, both focused on variations of the fatherly role, Zambra is in many ways declaring that we need to rethink the assumptions surrounding men's roles in the world and in literature.

In *My Documents*, that exploration becomes a radical, dark, tender, and at times brutal interrogation of the various masculine roles and expectations that have been passed down through generations. A book ahead of its time, it seems to prefigure our current moment, which among many other social ills is suffering from an oft-cited "crisis of masculinity." Father, son, teacher, friend, writer, reader—what do those words really mean? And what do they mean when we put the most basic adjectives like "good" and "bad" in front of them? What does it mean to be a "good man"?

The stories in this book center on male protagonists who are no heroes. They are often middle-class, mediocre men. Teachers who overstep in their positions of authority, angry divorced dads half-assing fatherhood, and, as in "Family Life," liars straight-up lying to lovers about who they even are. In the nesting-doll story "Artist's Rendition," a writer exploits a story of sexual assault to complete a commission, while a separate narrator wrestles with the moral implications of telling a tale whose reality he cannot comprehend. It is a demanding story in many respects—it takes some of the questions about authorial responsibility posited in *Ways of*

Going Home and spins them out to their darkest lengths. *My Documents*, in fact, is the book where Zambra arguably asks the most of the reader. In "Memories of a Personal Computer," for example, we as readers are implicated in turn when the protagonist on whose side we have so far uncomplicatedly been reveals himself capable of cold brutality. We feel betrayed, and also guilty for what our readerly complacencies have led us to accept in a character.

Other characters are more sympathetic in their ambivalent and bumbling searches for meaning, for a way to make room for tenderness and companionship within an often rigid definition of manhood. The character of Camilo seems to prefigure Vicente in *Chilean Poet*, both of them young men earnestly searching for a space of sincere and uncompetitive connection. And sure, Rodrigo (possibly the world's most Chilean man) makes his version of a grand gesture of love without realizing that it obliterates the agency of his beloved, but you can't help but admire his guts and feel a little sorry for him, though even that pity is not uncomplicated.

Zambra has said that all literature is fundamentally about belonging. I think what he means is that through literature, we as writers and readers come to understand our position in the world and our relationships with other humans. I can't help but think that this belonging also has much to do with compassion. And of course, we cannot talk about belonging without asking certain questions: "To what do we belong? To what do we *want* to belong?"

My Documents is, at its core, a book about what it means to belong to a gender that men are only recently having to start thinking of as a gender, a category to which one belongs, rather than a default state of human existence around which all other conditions are organized. In the story that opens the collection (the only straightforwardly autobiographical piece), the narrator looks back at his childhood, when he was awakening to Capital Letter subjects like Religion, Sexuality, Politics, and Literature. He tells us: "I tried to take positions, though they were, at first, erratic and fleeting, a bit like Leonard Zelig: what I wanted was to fit in, to belong . . . I figured out that a very effective way to belong was to simply keep quiet."

Silence is an important concept throughout Zambra's work. The idea of literature as bonsai, which he introduced in his first novel, has much to say (or not say) about it—the trimming away of all that is unnecessary or extraneous is also an injection of silence. There is the silence of complicity and the silence of fear in the years of the Pinochet dictatorship (most of the '70s and '80s) in both *Multiple Choice* and *Ways of Going Home*. And *My Documents* in its own way arises from a silence, the silence of processing, of self-criticism, where the "self" is an individual, yes, but also a group, a generational and often gendered "we." *My Documents* is an attempt to move out of that silence and to face, perhaps even change, that category of belonging we call masculinity.

Zambra, like many great writers, I suspect, is a person for whom language is a problem. Words don't say what we want them to, and that is a problem. Figuring out how to use words in a way that changes their meaning is a fundamental concern. Using them in a way that changes reality, even more so. In "Long Distance," the narrator uses letter writing to help his students "discover the power of language, the ability of words to truly influence reality." Later, similarly, *Chilean Poet* will find a protagonist frustrated with the negative connotations of the Spanish word for "stepfather," *padrastro*. But these are the words that we have, and "we have to use them. We have to use them or maybe invent others."

When *Ways of Going Home* established the idea of "literature of the children" (stories of those who grew up under dictatorship), it had much to do with the distrust or rejection of inherited literary voices and their version of "truth" that could tend toward the binary. Zambra was planting his flag in the territory in between, a no-man's-land from which to question the firm, sure, declarative voice that could also be dictatorial, paternalistic, patronizing, and didactic. More honest was an experimentalism that exposed not just the content but the container (as with a bonsai, a word that encompasses both tree and vessel), or, in *My Documents*, that put the machinery out in the open and emphasized the tools of writing. For computers are personal, which is to say individual. At least, the mass-manufactured screens we sit in front of create the illusion of individuality, and the trappings of capitalism work hard to encourage that illusion. Windows (which used to be mere panes of glass) comes with standardized folders that sound like selfish toddlers screaming "mine!" Because that "My Documents" folder is *yours*, no matter that every other computer comes with one just like it. The gesture of *My Documents* the book is to break out of that false or imposed individuality and move toward a deliberate "ours."

The passage from "Literature of the Children" to "Children's Literature"—as the title of Zambra's latest book, published in Spanish in 2023, might be transliterated—has been the search for a true, genuine narrative voice. In *My Documents*, that quest reached into dark depths and up to bright heights to articulate Zambra's most searching questions.

They are questions he has ventured answers to in his later books, but there is power and urgency in returning to the questions and seeing where we fit into them today.

I'm also pleased that we were able to include some additional stories in this edition, which we believe add to the book's range of meaning while not straying too far from its narrative scope. Some, like "Fantasy" and "Cyclops," were written well before the original publication of *My Documents*—"Fantasy," in fact, is one of Zambra's first short stories—while others were written later. They have all been published in English in various magazines, but have never been collected in a book before now. Still, every time I read "Penultimate Activities" I think it was there from the very beginning, as the perfect final piece for this volume.

As someone who has had Alejandro's voice in my head for well over a decade now, I am also a person for whom words are a problem. I can't help but notice how the words we often use to talk about translation tend to be fundamentally static: preserve, maintain, conserve. But what I hope to achieve in translation has more to do with a living text, one that makes room for you, our readers, the way I feel Zambra's writing has made room for me. Because while we may not be part of the same categories of belonging in terms of nationality or gender, in *My Documents*, Zambra is working to articulate a truly comprehensive empathy and shared sense of humanity.

MEGAN MCDOWELL
June 2023

My Documents

Part 1

My Documents

for Natalia García

1

The first time I saw a computer was in 1980, when I was four or five years old. It's not a pure memory, though—I'm probably mixing it up with other, later visits to my father's office, on Calle Agustinas in downtown Santiago.

I remember my father explaining how those enormous machines worked, his black eyes fixed on mine, his perpetual cigarette in hand. He waited for my awed reaction and I feigned interest, but as soon as I could, I went off to play at the desk of Loreto, a thin-lipped, big-haired secretary who never remembered my name.

Loreto's electric typewriter struck me as marvelous, with its small screen where the words accumulated until a powerful salvo carved them into the paper. The mechanism was perhaps similar to a computer, but I never thought of it that way. In any case, I preferred the other machine at her desk, a conventional black Olivetti, a model I was very familiar with because we had one just like it at my house. My mother had studied programming, but she'd abandoned computers and opted instead for that lesser technology, which was still current then, since computers hadn't yet been mass-marketed.

My mother's typing wasn't for any remunerated job: she transcribed songs, stories, and poems written by my grandmother, who was always entering some contest or working on a project that would, she thought, finally pull her out of anonymity and into the spotlight. I remember my mother working at the dining room table, carefully inserting the carbon paper, painstakingly applying Wite-Out when she made a mistake. She always typed fast, using all of her fingers, without looking at the keys.

Maybe I can put it this way: my father was a computer and my mother was a typewriter.

2

I soon learned how to type my name, but I preferred to use the keys to imitate the drumrolls of military marches. Becoming a member of the marching band was the greatest honor we could hope for. Everyone wanted to join, including me. At midmorning, during classes, we would hear the far-off bursts of the snare drums, the whistles, the exhalations of the trumpet and the trombone, the miraculously sharp notes of the triangle and the bells. The band practiced two or three times a week: I loved to watch as they marched off in formation toward the practice field at the edge of the school grounds. Most eye-catching of all was the drum major, who only appeared at important events because he was an alumnus of the school. He wielded his baton with admirable finesse, in spite of the fact that he only had one eye: one of his eyes was glass, and legend had it that he'd lost it due to a badly timed baton maneuver.

In December, we would make a pilgrimage to the Votive Temple of Maipú. It was an endless two-hour walk from the school, the marching band in front and the rest of us following behind, in descending order, from the thirteenth grade (because it was a technical high school) down to first. People came out to greet us, and some of the women gave us oranges to ward off exhaustion. My mother would appear at certain points along the way: she'd park somewhere, find me at the end of the column, then go back to the car to listen to music, smoke a cigarette, and drive another stretch to catch up with us farther on and wave at me again. With her long, shiny, brown hair, she was hands down the most beautiful mother of my class, which was something of a problem for me, because my classmates liked to tell me that she was too pretty to be the mom of someone as ugly as me.

Dante would also come out to support me; he belted my name at the top of his lungs and embarrassed me in front of my classmates, who made fun of him, and me. Dante was an autistic boy, older than me, maybe fifteen or sixteen. He was very tall, around six foot two, and weighed over 220 pounds, as he himself, for a time, would tell anyone he met, always giving the exact figure: "Hi, today I weigh 227 pounds."

Dante used to spend his days wandering around the neighborhood, trying to figure out which kids belonged to which parents, and who was whose sibling or friend, which, in a world where silence and suspicion reigned, couldn't have been easy. He would always approach his interlocutors from behind, and they would start walking faster, but then Dante would speed up, too, until he was facing them and walking backward, nodding his head sharply whenever he understood something. He lived with an aunt; apparently he'd been abandoned by his parents, but he never said that—when you asked him about his parents, he just gave you a disconcerted look.

3

On top of the afternoon marches I heard at school, I heard even more martial rhythms once I got home—we lived behind the Santiago Bueras Stadium, where the marching bands from other schools came to practice, and where occasionally, maybe once a month, there was a marching band competition. So I listened to military marches every day; you could say that they were the soundtrack of my childhood. But that would only be partially true: many kinds of music were important to my family. My grandmother had been an opera singer as a teenager, and her greatest disappointment in life was that she'd had to stop singing when she was twenty-one, when the earthquake of 1939 marked a before and after in her life. Who knows how many times she told us about that experience: how she'd choked on dirt, and woken up to suddenly find her city, Old Chillán, destroyed. The inventory of dead included her father, her mother, and two of her three brothers. It was that third brother who rescued her from the rubble.

My parents never told us bedtime stories, but my grandmother did. The happy stories would always end badly, because the protagonists invariably died in an earthquake. But she also told us some terribly sad stories that ended happily—maybe that was her idea of literature. Sometimes my grandmother would end up crying, and my sister and I would lie there awake, listening to her sobs; other times, even during an especially dramatic moment of the story, some detail would strike her as funny, and she'd burst out into peals of contagious laughter, and that would also keep us awake.

My grandmother was always coming up with double entendres or making impertinent comments that she cracked up at herself before she even finished them. She would say "butt of a horse" instead of "but of course," and if someone voiced the opinion that it was cold out, she would reply, "Well, it certainly isn't hot." She would also say "If we gotta fight 'em, let's bite 'em," and instead of simply saying "no," she was quick to reply "not at all, as the fish said," or just "as the fish said," or simply "fish," to summarize this saying: "not at all, as the fish said when asked how he'd like to be cooked, in the oven or the fryer."

4

Mass was held in the gymnasium of the Mater Purissima convent school, but people always talked about the church building that was in the works, and it was like they were describing a dream. It took so long to build that church that by the time it was finished, I no longer believed in God.

At first I went to mass with my parents, but I started going alone when they switched to the Ursuline school, which was closer and offered a mass that lasted only forty minutes, because the priest—a minuscule, bald man who always went around on a scooter—rushed through the homily, delivering it with amiable indifference; while he was talking he would often make a hand gesture that meant "et cetera." I liked him, but I preferred the priest at Mater Purissima, a man with a full, indomitable beard that was absolutely white. He spoke as though chastising or challenging us, employing many dramatic pauses and that energetic and deceptive friendliness that is so particular to priests. Of course, I also knew the priests at my school, like Father Limonta, the principal, a very athletic Italian—it was said he'd been a gymnast when he was younger—who gave us "love taps" with his ring of keys to keep us firmly in formation, and who otherwise was affable and fairly fatherly. His sermons, however, struck me as unpleasant or inappropriate—perhaps they seemed too pedagogical, unserious.

I liked the language of mass, but I didn't understand it very well. When we got to the part where we asked for forgiveness and said, "Through my fault, through my fault, through my most grievous fault," I mistook the word "fault" for "thought," and that strange insistence on the evils of thought made an impression that stayed with me. Then there was the sentence "I am not worthy to receive you," which I said once to my grandmother while opening the door. "I am not worthy to receive you in my house," I repeated the joke later to my father, who answered right away, with a sweet and severe smile: "Well, thank you, but this house is *mine*."

At Mater Purissima there was a chorus of six singers and two guitar players that had a starring role in the mass, because all the refrains, including the "Let us give thanks to God," and the "We praise you Lord," and even the "Hear us Lord, we beg you," were all sung. I aspired to join that choir. I was only eight years old, but I could play the little guitar we had at our house reasonably well: I strummed with a sense of rhythm, I could play scales, and though a nervous tremor overcame me when it was time to play a barre chord, I still got an almost-full sound out of it, only slightly impure. I guess I thought I was good, or good enough that I could, one morning after mass, guitar in hand, approach the members of the chorus. They looked down at me, perhaps because I was very small, or maybe because they were a fully functioning mafia, but they neither accepted nor rejected me. "We have to give you a tryout," said a blond woman with dark circles under her eyes who played an extraordinarily large guitar.

"Let's do it now," I proposed. I had some songs I'd practiced, among them the "Our Father," which was often sung to the tune of "The Sounds of Silence," but she refused.

"Next month," she told me.

5

My mother had grown up listening devotedly to the Beatles and a repertoire of Chilean folk music, and then she'd moved on to hits by Adamo, Sandro, Raphael, and José Luis Rodríguez, which was more or less what you heard on the radio at the beginning of the eighties. She had stopped looking for new music—or new to her—until she came across the album of Paul Simon and Art Garfunkel's reunion concert in Central Park. Her life changed then, I think forever: overnight, and with remarkable speed, the house filled with hard-to-find albums, and she took up studying English again, maybe just so she could understand the lyrics.

I remember her listening to the BBC English course—which came in binders that held dozens of cassette tapes—or to the other course we had in the house, "The Three Way

Method to English": two boxes, one red and the other green, each with a notebook, a book, and three LPs. I'd sit beside her and listen distractedly to those voices. I still remember some fragments, like the man who would say, "These are my eyes," and the woman who would reply, "Those are your eyes." The best part was when the masculine voice asked, "Is this the pencil?" and the woman answered, "No, this is not the pencil, but the pen," and then, when the man asked, "Is this the pen?" she answered, "No, this is not the pen, but the pencil."

I tend to think that every time I came home, some song by Simon & Garfunkel, or Paul Simon solo, was playing in the living room. By the time *Graceland* was released in 1986, my mother was definitely Simon's most fervent Chilean fan, not to mention how well versed she was in the singer's life; she could tell you all about his failed marriage to Carrie Fisher, for example, or his bit part in *Annie Hall*. My father was surprised that his wife had so suddenly become a fan of that music that he—who back then was listening exclusively to Argentine zambas—didn't like at all. "I should have my own room," I overheard my mother say one night, sobbing, after an argument set off by some posters and photos she'd brought home to hang in the master bedroom, provoking my father's ire. In the end, though, he had to resign himself to those images of other men looming over his marital bed.

6

On weekends in the spring, and even sometimes in summer, I went with my aunts and uncles and cousins to fly kites on Hill 15. It was all very professional: my father had progressed from hanging the kite string between two trees in order to treat it with crushed glass, like he did as a kid, to building a complex mechanism for home-treating the string by hooking up two big spools to a motor. He also made his own kites. Though I'm sure that back then he was also solving arduous computing dilemmas, when I think of my father at work, the image I see is of him on those nights, laboring over his attempts to achieve the perfect kite.

I didn't dislike kite flying, but I preferred to do it with regular string; I was incapable of handling the treated kite string without destroying my fingertips, even though they were already a little hardened from playing the guitar. But you had to use treated string, that was the point: you got the kite up in the sky and tried to take down your opponent. While my cousin Rodrigo sawed vigorously away, cutting down dozens of kites every afternoon, I usually had trouble even keeping my kite aloft, and I lost control of it on a regular basis. I went on trying, even though pretty soon no one held out much hope for me.

We always brought along a box holding dozens of splendid kites, the ones my dad made plus others we bought from a friend of his who made kites for a living. I always tried to find a spot as far away as possible from my family. Sometimes, instead of flying my kite, I would set it beside me and spend a couple of hours stretched out in the grass, smoking my first cigarettes while I watched the capricious trajectories of the cut kites as they fell. "How much for that one?" someone asked me on one of those afternoons. It was Mauricio, the altar boy. I sold him the kite, and soon I was selling others to his brother and his brother's friends.

Mauricio was so freckled it was funny just to look at him, but it had still taken me a moment to recognize him without his white robe. In my confusion, in my ignorance, I had thought that altar boys were very young priests, and that they all lived together in a cloister or something. He clarified that, no, they did not, and he told me that he preferred to be called an *acolyte* rather than an altar boy. He asked me if I wanted to serve at mass, because the other acolyte was about to retire. He wanted to know if I'd had my first communion, and for some reason I said I had, which was completely false—I was just starting the preparations at school. I wasn't even sure it was a requirement for being an altar boy, but instinctively, like so many other times in my life when I've been unsure, I lied. Then I told him I wasn't sure, but I'd think about it. When I went back to where my dad and my uncles were, I learned they had discovered my kite-selling business, but no one scolded me.

7

I was still waiting for the baggy-eyed woman to give me a tryout, but every time I asked her about it, she only made excuses. I remember I said, trying to impress her, that the English version of the "Our Father" was better. "It's impossible for anything to be better than the word of our lord Jesus Christ," she replied. But I must have piqued her curiosity, because when I was leaving, she asked me if I knew what the English version said. "It's about the sounds of silence," I told her, with utter certainty.

I got tired of waiting, and one or two weeks after running into Mauricio on Hill 15, I approached him and the priest and told them I wanted to be an acolyte. The priest peered at me suspiciously, inspecting me up and down before finally agreeing. I was happy. I wouldn't sing at mass, but I would have an even more prominent role. I wouldn't wear the white pants of the marching band, but I'd have the white robe with its stiff cord tied firmly around my waist. Mauricio could lend me the clothes. I didn't tell anyone at home that I was going to be an altar boy. I don't really know why, maybe I just didn't want them to come watch me.

8

The first time I served at mass, I spent the first few minutes sneaking vengeful glances at the blond musician, but she just sat there refusing to notice my triumph. It was hard to concentrate on the rituals that I normally respected and believed in, but which just then, up on stage, I barely seemed to remember. There were moments of glory, like when we rang the bells or seconded the priest in the sign of peace. But then the dreaded crossroads came: it was my turn to receive communion. My plan had been to tell the priest before mass that I couldn't take communion because I'd gone too long without confessing, but I had forgotten and now it was too late. I tried to make a gesture that communicated all of that, a gesture that would hopefully be imperceptible to the faithful behind me, but I couldn't—the priest stuffed the host in my mouth, and it tasted the way it does to everyone: bland. But at that moment I didn't care about the taste—I thought I was going to die right there, struck down by a bolt of lightning or something. I walked home with Mauricio and I considered confessing my sin to him, but he was so happy, congratulating me over and over again on my performance at mass, that I didn't mention it.

When we got to Mauricio's house, which was close to

Mater Purissima, his older brother invited me to have lunch with them—their parents were out. We ate charquicán and listened to Pablo Milanés, whom I knew for his song "Años," which I thought was funny, and also for "El breve espacio en que no estás," which I liked. Using a double tape deck, Mauricio and his brother had recorded each song on the album three times in a row on a 90-minute tape, or maybe it was 120 minutes ("They're so good you want to listen to them again right away," Mauricio explained to me).

The brothers sang along in horrible voices while they ate; they yelled the lyrics unabashedly, even with their mouths full, which I appreciated. When someone sang off-key in my grandmother's presence, she would whisper as though telling a secret (but loud enough that everyone could hear), things like: "It's clear that we aren't at the Opera," or "Someone woke up out of tune today," or "Does this soprano have a mustache?" But my grandmother wasn't there to reprimand those brothers who sang with utter abandon, with ease: you could tell they had sung those songs an infinite number of times, and the music meant something important to them.

While we spooned our ice cream, I started paying attention to the lyrics of "Acto de fe": "Creo en ti, como creo cuando crece / cuanto se siente y padece." The end of the lyrics struck me as disconcerting: I'd thought it was a love song, but it ended with the word "revolution." The brothers sang with all their hearts: "I believe in you, revolution."

I was eight years old, or maybe nine by then, and although I was a boy who liked words, that was the first time I ever heard the word "revolution." I asked Mauricio if it was a name, because I thought it might refer to the singer's beloved: Revolution González, for instance, or Revolution Smith.

They laughed and looked at me indulgently. "It's not a name," Mauricio's brother clarified. "Revolution? You really don't know that word? Well, then you're a turd."

I knew it was a joke, mostly because it rhymed. Then Mauricio's brother gave me a class on Chilean and Latin American history that I wish I could recall to the letter, but all I remember is the feeling of growing bewilderingly and uncomfortably aware of my own ignorance. I knew nothing about the world, nothing. The brother left, and Mauricio and I went to watch TV in his bedroom; we fell asleep or half asleep. We started to grope each other, to touch each other all over, without kissing. Throughout all our years of friendship, we never did that again, nor did we ever mention it.

9

I arrived home just after dark. I wasn't in the habit of praying, but that night I did, for a long time—I needed God's help. In just one day I had accumulated two tremendous sins, although I was more worried about my false communion than my dalliance with Mauricio.

My grandmother saw me there, kneeling in front of a portrait of Christ that was hanging in the living room, and she couldn't hold back her laughter. I asked what she was laughing at, and she told me not to exaggerate, that one "Our Father" would get the job done. My grandmother never went to mass: she said the priests were too nosy, but she did believe in God. "There's no need to say prayers," she explained that night. "It's enough to have a conversation with Jesus, freely, before going to sleep." I thought that was strange, or at least intimidating.

Although I went to a Catholic school, I didn't associate any religious sentiment with what went on there. I didn't like it when they made us go to mass at school, or to those tedious sessions in the church adjoining the main building where they prepared us for our first communion—those stupid lists of questions, as if we were memorizing traffic rules. But at recess the next morning, I decided that even though I hadn't had my first communion yet, I needed to confess, or at least talk to a priest about my sins, so I set off for Father Limonta's office. He was absorbed in an account book, balancing some numbers, I guess. When he raised his head he gave me a severe look, and I froze stiff. "I already know why you're here," he said, and I started trembling, imagining the priest had some kind of direct back channel with God. I went blank, felt dizzy. "It's not going to happen," Limonta said finally. "All the kids come in here and ask the same thing, but you're still too young for the band." I ran out, relieved, and went back to class.

I think it was that same day when the head teacher and a priest whose name I don't remember brought us to a home for mentally challenged children. The goal of the visit was to show us just how fortunate we were, and there was even a script to increase the drama: one by one the children would approach the teacher, who would say kind things: "You mean so much to us, Jonathan." But the teacher did not hug or touch the children, there was no physical affection. The children, who had twisted mouths, skewed eyes, snot hanging from their noises, would mumble something incomprehensible in response. Each case was more heartrending than the last, and the final person to be paraded out was Lucy, a forty-year-old woman with a little girl's body, who seemed paralyzed but would turn her head when the priest rang a bell. I remember I thought about Dante, who was normal compared to those kids, even though in our neighborhood they called him "the mongoloid."

Up until then, my idea of suffering had been associated with Dante and the handicapped children on the telethon, which was an inexhaustible font of fears and nightmares. Every year my sister and I, like nearly all children, would watch the entire program until we were falling-down tired, and then we would spend weeks imagining what it would be like to lose our arms or legs.

10

"This is nothing," my grandmother said after the 1985 earthquake, hugging me. We went back to school some months later, and they switched us to a temporary classroom they'd constructed behind the gym, where we stayed for the rest of the year.

We had a new teacher, too. The first thing he told us was his name, Juan Luis Morales Rojas, and he repeated it in a quiet voice, in a neutral tone, two, three, twenty times. "Now you all repeat it," he told us, "Juan Luis Morales Rojas," and we started to repeat his name, with growing confidence, louder and louder, trying to understand if there was a limit to how loud we could be, and after a while we were shouting and jumping while he moved his hands like an orchestra director, or like a musician who was enjoying listening to the audience sing along to the chorus of one of his songs. "Now I know you're never going to forget my name," was all he said when we finally got tired of shouting and laughing. In all my years at that school, I don't remember a happier moment than that one. Weeks later, or maybe that same day, Juan Luis Morales Rojas told us what elections were, what the president's duties were, and what the vice president, the secretary, and the treasurer all did. In one of the first Class Council sessions, the two-hour meetings we would have on Mondays, Rojas asked us to make a list of all the problems we had, and at first we couldn't think of anything, but then someone mentioned how fourth graders weren't allowed in the band. The idea arose to make a list of all the kids who wanted to be in the band, and then go and talk with Father Limonta. I was going to raise my hand, but I hesitated. Then I realized, quite clearly, that no, I didn't want to be in the band.

11

After a while, my mom ran into a woman who was sure she had seen me serving at mass. "That's impossible," my mother replied. But then someone else told her the same thing, and she asked me about it again. I told her the person was wrong, but that I had also seen someone who looked surprisingly like me acting as altar boy. "I just have a very common face," I told her.

When I finally did go to confession with Father Limonta, it didn't even occur to me to tell him that I had already taken communion, or to mention my erotic experience with Mauricio. Later I received my first communion at school—which was actually my thirtieth or fortieth—and I could finally take it legitimately at mass.

My parents were there and they gave me presents, and I think that was when I felt the true weight of my double life.

I went on serving at Mater Purissima without my parents' knowledge, until maybe the winter of 1985, when, after a tense and sloppy mass, the priest criticized us harshly: he told us we distracted him, that we were too shrill, that we had no rhythm. His comments hit me hard, maybe because I was precariously coming to understand that the priest was acting, that it wasn't all enlightenment, or whatever you call that sacred vocation, that spiritual dimension. I decided to quit, and at that very moment, I stopped being Catholic. I guess that's also when all my religious feeling was entirely extinguished. I never had, in any case, those rational meditations on the existence of God, maybe because I started to believe, naively, intensely, absolutely, in literature.

12

After the attempt on Pinochet's life, in September of '86, Dante started asking everyone in the neighborhood if they belonged to the right or the left. Some of the neighbors seemed uncomfortable, others laughed and started walking even faster, and still others asked him what he understood as left and right. But he never asked us kids, only the adults.

I stayed friends with Mauricio and we still listened to Milanés at his house, but more often to Silvio Rodríguez, Violeta Parra, Inti-Illimani, and Quilapayún, and I still got lessons from him and his brother about revolution and communal labor. It was from them that I first heard about the victims of the dictatorship, about the people who'd been arrested and disappeared, the murders, the torture. I listened to them perplexed. Sometimes I got mad at them, and other times I fell prey to a certain skepticism, but I was always filled with the same feeling of illegitimacy, of ignorance, smallness, and estrangement.

I tried to take positions, though they were, at first, erratic and fleeting, a bit like Leonard Zelig: what I wanted was to fit in, to belong, and if they were on the left, I wanted to be, too, the same way I wanted to be on the right at home, even though my parents weren't really right-wing. It was more that politics were never mentioned in my house, except when my mother complained about how hard it had been to get milk for my sister during Salvador Allende's government.

I figured out that a very effective way to belong was to simply keep quiet. I figured out, or began to figure out, that the news actually hid reality, and that I was part of a conformist crowd neutralized by television. My idea of suffering became the image of a child who lived in fear of his parents' being murdered, or who grew up without ever knowing them except through a few black-and-white photographs. Even though I did everything I could to distance myself from my parents, the idea of losing them was, for me, the most devastating thing imaginable.

13

"It's not about remembering / the first communion / but rather the last," says a poem by Claudio Giaconi. I'm wrapping up now.

14

At the beginning of 1987 the Pope came to Chile, and I felt that old religious fervor coming back, but it didn't last long.

At the end of that same year, just days after I had turned twelve, I found out I was going to be sent to a new school. I hadn't exactly become a virtuosic guitar player, but I had my moment of musical glory when I won the school's talent show by singing "El baile de los que sobran," by Los Prisioneros. The boy who got second place sang, in a perfect and melodious voice, "Detenedla ya" by Emmanuel. I have no idea how I beat him. My voice was starting to change, I had trouble hitting the right notes. And I didn't know what I was singing. I didn't know what I was singing.

In March of 1988 I entered the National Institute. And that's when, at the same time, democracy and adolescence arrived. The adolescence was real. The democracy wasn't.

In 1994 I began studying literature at the University of Chile. There was a shiny black computer in my house. Every once in a while I used it to write my papers or type poems that I then printed out, but I always erased the files. I didn't want to leave any records.

At the end of 1997 I was living in a boardinghouse across from the National Stadium, and I had completely fallen out with my father. I wouldn't take his money, but I did accept a used laptop that he insisted on giving me. And even if he hadn't insisted, I still would have accepted it. It was fitting that my favorite album then was called *OK Computer*. I wrote while listening to "No Surprises" a thousand times, and I wrote about everything except for my family, because back then I pretended I didn't have a one. No family, no house, no past. Sometimes I also listened to "I Am a Rock," by Simon & Garfunkel, and that was also appropriate, because that's how I lived, that's what I thought, gravely, with absolute faith: "I have my books / and my poetry to protect me."

In 1999 the laptop my father had given me—a black IBM with a little red ball in the middle of the keyboard that served as a mouse (which the IT guys called "the clitoris")—broke down definitively. I bought, in many monthly installments, an immense Olidata. By then I was living at Vicuña Mackenna 58, in the basement apartment of a big old building. I was working as a night phone operator, and in the afternoons, I wrote and looked out the window at the legs and shoes of people walking by on Eulogia Sánchez. That winter, because I didn't have a heater or a hot-water bottle, I spent several nights sleeping with my arms around the computer.

In 2005 the use of treated kite string was outlawed due to the number of accidents it caused, and to the grisly case of a motorcyclist who'd been killed by one some years before. But by then my father had already moved on to fly fishing.

In August of 2008, my grandmother died. Just a few days ago, my mother and I went through her stories, which my mom had long since transferred to the computer, in Comic Sans MS font, 12 point, double-spaced. I knew the beginning of "Ninette" by heart: "This is a story about a family whose noble lineage made them more high-and-mighty every day, except for the daughter, an only child, who stood out for being good and kind."

Today is July 5, 2013. My mother no longer has posters hanging in the conjugal bedroom, but she still follows Paul Simon. This morning, over the phone, we talked about him, about what his life must be like now, and whether he has found happiness with Edie Brickell. I assured her he has, because I'm pretty sure I'd be happy with Edie Brickell, too.

It's nighttime, it's always nighttime when the story ends. I reread, rephrase sentences, specify names. I try to remember better: more, and better. I cut and paste, change and enlarge the font, play with line spacing. I think about closing this file and leaving it forever in the My Documents folder. But I'm going to publish it, I want to, even though it's not finished, even though it's impossible to finish it.

My father was a computer, my mother a typewriter.

I was a blank page, and now I am a book.

Part 2

Camilo

I t's Camilo!" he shouted to me from the gate, opening his arms wide, as if we knew each other. "Your daddy's god-son." It seemed terribly suspicious to me, like a caricature of danger, and I was nine then, already too big to fall for a trap like that. Those dark glasses, like a blind man's, and on such a cloudy day. And that jean jacket, covered in sewn-on patches with the names of rock bands. "My dad's not here," I told him, closing the door, and I didn't even tell my father he'd come by. I forgot.

But it turned out to be true: my dad had been a close friend of Camilo's father, Big Camilo—they'd played soccer to-gether on the Renca team. We had photographs of Little Camilo's baptism, the baby crying and the adults looking sol-emnly into the camera. All was well for several years—my father was an engaged godfather, and he took an interest in the child—but he and Big Camilo had a fight, and later, some months after the coup, Big Camilo was imprisoned, and after he was released he went into exile. The plan was for his wife, July, to bring Little Camilo and meet up with him in Paris, but she changed her mind, and in fact the marriage ended. So Little Camilo grew up missing his father, waiting for him, saving up money to go visit him. And one day, just after he turned eighteen, he decided that if he couldn't see his father, he should at least find his godfather.

I learned all this the first time Camilo came to have dinner with us, or maybe I found it out gradually. I want to be clear here, and I'm getting confused. But I remember how my father was moved that day when he saw how much his godson resembled his old friend. "You have his face," he told Camilo, which was not necessarily a compliment, because it was an unremarkable face, difficult to remember, and though Camilo used all kinds of products to try to style his woolly hair, it had a tendency to play dirty tricks on him.

Despite my initial distrust, I quickly learned that Camilo was one of the most entertaining people imaginable. He soon became a benevolent and protective presence, a luminous person who was a real older brother to me. When he went off to France to fulfill his lifelong dream, that's what I felt, that I was losing my brother. It was January of 1991; that I can say for certain.

I wasn't the only one who was fascinated by Camilo. My older sister was completely infatuated, and my younger sister, who usually couldn't keep her attention on anything for more than two seconds, would watch him intently when he came to visit, laughing at every one of his wisecracks. Not to mention my mom, whom he joked around with but also spoke to seriously, because during that time Camilo was—in his own words—full of religious doubt, and although my mother was no zealot, she was so astounded by the idea that a person could deny the existence of God that she'd sit and listen to him in awe.

As for my father, I think that Camilo became more of a friend to him than a godson; he even let Camilo address him with the informal *tú*. They would sit up late in the living room, talking about all kinds of things—except the existence of God, because my father didn't allow such things to be questioned, or soccer, because Camilo was the first male I ever met who didn't like soccer. I adored it, and Camilo's obliviousness seemed funny and exotic to me. He didn't even understand the rules. The only match he'd ever played took place in the San Miguel gym, when he was five years old: his knowledge of the game back then came from the goals he'd seen replayed on TV, so he spent the whole afternoon running around randomly, cheering for goals that hadn't happened and waving happily to the fans, utterly uninterested in the ball.

My own relationship with my father, however, was closely tied to soccer. We watched or listened to games together, sometimes went to the stadium, and every Sunday at noon I went with him to a field in La Farfana, where he played goalie. He was really good—I remember him as though suspended in the air, grabbing hold of the ball with both hands and clutching it to his chest. Still, I always suspected that his teammates hated him, because he was the kind of goalie who spent the whole game barking instructions, ordering around the defense, and even the midfield players, at the top of his lungs. "Pass it back, man, pass it back! Here! Pass it back, man, back!" How many times did I hear my father shout those words in a tone of utmost alarm. When he yelled at me—if he ever did—it was never as loud as those shrieks on the soccer field. His teammates put up with him in annoyance, or at least that's what I assumed, since trying to play with that nonstop commotion in the background can't have been pleasant. But he was respected, my father. And I'll say it again: he was really good. I would settle in behind the goal with my Bilz soda or a Chocolito ice cream bar, and sometimes he would glance over at me to be sure I was still there, and other times he would ask me, without turning around, what had happened, because that was my father's main problem as a goalie, the reason he never went pro: his myopia was so severe that he could see only as far as the midfield. His reflexes, however, were extraordinary, as was his bravery, which he paid for with two fractures in his right hand and one in his left.

During halftime I liked to go and stand in the goalie's spot, and invariably I'd think about how immense the goal was. Over and over, I wondered how anyone could possibly block a penalty kick. My father blocked penalty kicks—of course he did. One out of every three or four: he never dived for them early, he always waited, and if the execution was anything less than perfect, he blocked it.

✦ ✦ ✦ ✦ ✦

I remember a trip to the country, when Camilo discovered that I blinked between streetlights. I still do it, even when I'm driving; I can't help it. As soon as I get on the highway, I start blinking carefully, trying to hit the exact midpoint between lights. That day, my sisters, Camilo, and I were crowded into the backseat of my parents' Chevette, and Camilo noticed that I was tense, concentrating, and then he started to blink at the same time that I did, smiling at me. I got worried, because I didn't want to make any mistakes; I fervently believed that only if I blinked between streetlights would we all be kept safe.

My nervous habits don't bother me so much now, but when I was a kid they used to make me so anxious that even the simplest activities became unbearable. I guess I was partly or completely OCD. Like many children, I scrupulously avoided the cracks in the sidewalk. If I ever accidentally stepped on one, I fell into a state of unspeakable despair—and yet I knew, on some level, that it was all too ridiculous to talk about. I also had an obsession with balancing out parts of my body: if one leg hurt, I'd hit the other one to make them even. Sometimes I'd move my right shoulder to the rhythm of my heartbeat, as if I had two hearts. I had predilections for certain numbers and colors, as well, and some truly random routines, like going nine times up and down the steep staircase that led from the pool to the park. This wasn't really so strange, it could even have been a kind of game, but I kept it from being one by hiding it carefully: I'd stop at the bottom step, shake my head as if I'd forgotten something, and then turn around and retrace my steps.

If I mention all this it's only because Camilo always seemed willing to help me. That time in the Chevette, when he realized how nervous I was, he patted my hair and said something I don't remember, but I'm sure that it was warm, caring, and subtle. Sometime later, when I opened up to him about my weird habits, he told me that everyone was different, and maybe the strange things I did were normal, or maybe they weren't, but it didn't matter, because normal people sucked.

————

I could fill many pages writing about Camilo's importance in my life. For now, I remember that it was Camilo who, after many long and sophisticated arguments, managed to get me permission to go to my first concert. (We saw Aparato Raro at the Don Orione school in Cerrillos.) He was also the first person to read my poems. I'd written poems since I was little, which was, of course, a shameful secret. They weren't any good, but I thought they were, and when Camilo read them he was respectful, though he immediately explained that these days poems didn't rhyme. That was news to me. I had never read a poem that didn't rhyme, and I'd always thought that poetry was something unchanging, ancient and immutable. But it was great to hear, since there were times when I bent over backward to find rhymes, and I knew I couldn't always fall back on the easy combinations.

I asked him what the difference was, then, between a poem and a story. We were stretched out by the Maipú municipal pool—in full-on photosynthesis, as he would say. He looked at me with a pedagogical expression and told me that a poem was the exact opposite of a story. "Stories are boring. Poetry is madness, poetry is savage, poetry is a torrent of extreme emotions," he said, or something like that. It's difficult not to start inventing, not to let myself be carried along on the scent of memory. He definitely used the words "madness," "savage," and "emotions." "Torrent," maybe not. I think "extreme," yes.

Back at home, he picked up my notebook and started to write poems himself. It took him maybe half an hour to write ten or twelve long texts, and then he read them to me. I didn't understand a thing. I asked if other people understood his poems. He told me that people might not understand them, but that wasn't the important thing. I asked him if he wanted to publish a book. He said yes, he was sure he would, but that wasn't the important thing, either. I asked him what the important thing was. And he said this, or this was what I took away: "The important thing is to express your feelings, to demonstrate that you're a passionate, interesting man, maybe a bit fragile, someone who isn't afraid of anything, someone who accepts his feminine side." That was definitely the first time I heard the expression "feminine side."

Another day, not long after that, he asked me if I liked men or women. I was a little alarmed, because there were certainly guys that I liked—Camilo himself, for example— but I was quite sure that I liked girls more, much more. "I like girls," I told him. "I like them a lot. I think they're hot as hell."

"Okay," he said, very seriously, perhaps not entirely convinced, and then he added that if I liked guys it was all right—that happened sometimes, too.

I remember Camilo that afternoon standing on the bow-shaped bridge in Providencia, smoking. I could tell it was not your usual cigarette, but I didn't know exactly what it was. "It's too strong for a kid," he said in apology when I asked him for a drag, because by then I'd started smoking once in a while. This must have been 1986 or early 1987; I was ten or eleven years old. I know because at that age I still couldn't find my way around Providencia or downtown Santiago very well, and also because later that day we went to buy *True Stories* by Talking Heads, which was still a new album then.

"We have to solve your problem," Camilo had told me that morning as we were walking toward the bus stop. I asked him which problem, because I thought I had a lot, not just one. "Your shyness," he replied. "Girls don't like shy guys." And I really was shy back then; I'm talking about genuine shyness, not the kind you see now, when everyone is supposedly shy and it's become almost a joke. If someone doesn't say hi, it's because he's shy; if a guy kills his wife, it's because of shyness; if he defrauds a whole town, if he runs for office, if he eats the last bit of Nutella from the jar without asking anyone: shy. No, I'm talking about something else: stuttering, insecurity, introspection, not to mention those little tics of mine.

"I'm going to help you," Camilo told me. "I'm going to give you a lesson, but don't worry, you won't have to do anything—just stick with me, don't leave my side no matter what I do." I nodded, feeling a bit dizzy. During the hour-long bus ride, he told me jokes, mostly ones he'd told me before, but this time he told them in a very loud voice, all but shouting. I thought the lesson was that I had to laugh just as loud, which was very hard for me, but I tried. Then, as we were getting off the bus, he told me that that had not been the lesson.

We went up onto the bridge and stopped halfway across. Camilo smoked in silence, while I looked down at the murky, rushing water of the river, which was higher than usual. I focused on the current until I was so concentrated that I had the feeling the water was standing still and we were aboard a moving boat, although I'd never been on a boat in my life. I stayed like that for a long time, fifteen, maybe twenty minutes. "We're on a boat," I said to Camilo. I had trouble explaining;

he didn't get it, but then, suddenly, he saw it, too, and he let out a cry of profound astonishment. We went on gazing at the current while he repeated, "Amazing, amazing, amazing."

Afterward, as we were walking toward Providencia, he told me ceremoniously, "I've always liked you a lot, I still do, but now you have gained my respect." When we reached an intersection, maybe Providencia and Carlos Antúnez, he looked at me, gave a subtle, sharp nod that meant *now*, then threw himself to the ground, clutching his stomach, and started laughing extravagantly, scandalously. A group of people gathered around us right away, and I did not want to be there, but I understood that this was the lesson. When he finally stopped laughing, five policemen were there asking for an explanation. Camilo gave me another nod, this time of approval—I had stayed beside him the whole time, and I had even laughed a little, too, as though I were the laugher's shy friend, sure, but I wasn't so shy as to be embarrassed. I watched the cops' faces, impassive and severe, while Camilo rattled off a disjointed explanation in which he talked about me and my shyness, and how it was necessary to teach me this lesson so that I could, he told them, grow. He had disrupted the public order, we were living under a dictatorship, but Camilo managed to placate the policemen, and we walked away after making the strange promise never to laugh in a public place again.

"I'm really high," Camilo told me, or maybe he said it to himself, a little concerned. We went to a mall to buy the Talking Heads album. The record store seemed different from any I'd been to before—everything seemed luxurious and exclusive. When the salesclerk handed us *True Stories*,

Camilo translated the opening lyrics of "Love for Sale," though he may have improvised a little, since he didn't know any English. I took the album from him, examined its splendid red-and-white cover, and then I gave him the same quick nod he'd given me: *now*. He barely had time to acknowledge it with a panicked look before I took off with the record in my hands, and we went running, dodging pedestrians at full speed, for a long time, laughing like crazy.

That evening, there was a Colo-Colo soccer match on TV—I don't remember who they were playing—and Camilo stayed to watch it with us. My dad asked him why. "I don't have a father," Camilo said. "You're my godfather, so you have to teach me about soccer. Otherwise," he warned, winking at me, "I'll turn out to be a fairy."

It became routine for Camilo to watch the games with us, but I don't know if my dad enjoyed it. The questions Camilo asked were so simple and clueless that, before long, it got tedious.

On December 4, 1987, I committed a mortal sin. Los Prisioneros had just released *La cultura de la basura*, their third album; I was dying to buy it, but I didn't have a single peso. I considered stealing again, but I didn't think I could do it—that time with Talking Heads had been a spontaneous flash of inspiration. Then I had a better idea: since the album's release coincided with the annual telethon, I asked my parents for money to help the handicapped children, and then I headed off to the store and bought the cassette.

I felt awful. I locked myself in my room to listen to the tape, and at first every song sounded, in one way or another, as if it were about my act of villainy. I decided that I had to go to confession, but I was afraid of the priest's reaction. "Confess to me," Camilo said, when I told him I felt guilty. "What do you need to go blabbing your business to a priest for? Also, I'll tell you straight off: masturbating is not a sin. I think even Jesus whacked off a few times thinking about Mary Magdalene."

I laughed so much I felt giddy. Never in my life had I heard such heresy. There was a picture of Jesus above the table in the living room, and from then on I could never look at it without thinking that that was the face he made after ejaculating. Anyway, I had never thought that masturbation was a sin. When I told Camilo what I had done, he told me that the telethon met its goals through the sponsorships alone, and that maybe I had *needed* that cassette, maybe I had done the right thing. "I don't understand," I said.

"Okay, fine," he pronounced. "If you still feel guilty, pray that one prayer where you have to hit your chest."

"What about your godmother? Have you seen her?" I asked him one morning. In those days he often stayed over and slept in the living room, and he'd get up early and bring back a watermelon from the market, because it was summer. He said yes, that his godmother was still his mother's best friend.

"How about you? Do you have godparents?"

"Yeah, my aunt and uncle, my mom's brother and sister."

"That's no good," he said. "The idea is that they aren't family. Aunts and uncles will give you presents anyway. I think my dad should be your godfather," he told me very seriously.

"When I go see him I'm going to ask him to be your godfather. I promise."

Camilo still insisted that we teach him about soccer, and sometimes we practiced penalty kicks in the street. But my father would get fed up; he said that Camilo didn't concentrate, that he didn't take it seriously. Still, one weekend, the three of us went to Santa Laura Stadium to watch a doubleheader. First up was University of Chile against Concepción. Camilo, to the great annoyance of my father and me, had decided to root for the U, which had been his father's team, although of course he didn't even know the players' names. He liked how everyone in the stadium criticized and shouted at the players, but was surprised to see that they got angry with the ref. He decided to come to his defense, and although at first people didn't take it well, it was truly funny to hear Camilo, every time the ref called a foul or carded a player, stand up and yell, "Very well done, sir! Excellent decision!"

Camilo kept cheering on the referee during the next match, which was between Colo-Colo and Naval, I think. I joined him for a while, even though watching Colo-Colo was for me a very serious matter. I had grown up admiring Chino Hisis, Pillo Vera, Carlos Caszely, Horacio Simaldone, and of course Roberto Rojas—"el Cóndor." I had hated some players, too: Cristián Saavedra (I don't know why) and Mario Osbén, but only during the period when the coach inexplicably made Osbén and Rojas alternate as starters. That infuriated me. One of the great joys of my childhood was going down to the fence to yell at the coach, and I'd really let him have it. At home, cursing was strictly forbidden, but at the stadium I had free rein.

None of those guys were playing for Colo-Colo anymore that day at the stadium with Camilo, but the one I missed the most was obviously Cóndor Rojas. All Chileans admired Rojas, but for me, because he was a goalie, it was also a round-about way of admiring my father. What's more, I knew the position perfectly, and I considered the goalie's job to be without a doubt the hardest. Sometimes I played goalie, too, trying to emulate Cóndor Rojas, or maybe my father (in all but the shouting). Still, when I joined the Cobresal Youth leagues in Maipú, playing on the same field where Iván Zamorano began his career, I tried out as a midfielder and not a goalie. I was afraid, perhaps, that I wouldn't be good enough.

Why did Camilo spend so much time with us? Because we loved him, I'm sure. And because he didn't like being at his own house. He fought with his mother, often about his religious beliefs or the political situation. Before the 1988 referendum, Camilo went to all the demonstrations in favor of the "No" vote, which led to severe arguments. He wanted "No" to win because he hated Pinochet, but also because he thought that it would bring his father back to Chile. But Camilo's father didn't want to come back, or at least that's what Auntie July always told him: "Your dad has another family now. He has another country. He doesn't even remember you." But Camilo's dad still wrote to him, sent him money, and called him every once in a while.

Auntie July was tough. Even so, she treated us very well the one time I went with Camilo to their house. She gave us

bread cake and banana milk while we played Montezuma's
Revenge with Camilo's half brothers. It was strange to see
Camilo there. He didn't seem to belong. I went into his room,
and it was as if he didn't live there. He used to give my sisters
and me posters and decorations to hang on our walls, but
there was none of that in his own room: I was struck by those
white, empty walls, without even a nail to hang a photograph.

Oh, what did Camilo study? Administration or manage-
ment of something, at the Metropolitan University of Technology, which back then was called the Santiago Professional
Institute. But he didn't like to study. Once, he tried to give
me math lessons, but he wasn't very good at it. Nor do I know
if he read much, though I feel like he did. I think he'd mentioned Rimbaud, Baudelaire, and the poètes maudits that
time he talked to me about poetry. Or maybe it wasn't them,
but he did name some authors.

I often think, from this suspiciously stable place that is the
present, that Camilo was immature. But no. He wasn't. Or
he also had another side, an intuitive, generous, perceptive
side.

He was there with us, in front of the TV, when Cóndor
Rojas faked his injury in Brazil and the Chilean team walked
off the field at the Maracanã Stadium. My dad and I couldn't
believe what we were seeing, and Camilo was distraught, too.
"Fucking Brazilians!" I shouted, to see if I'd be scolded, but
no one scolded me. My father sank deep into a sad, furious
silence. Camilo immediately set off downtown, and he was
part of the crowd that protested in front of the Brazilian Em-
bassy. I wanted to go with him, but my parents wouldn't let
me, and I had to swallow my rage.

One evening, while the subject was still being discussed

and Cóndor Rojas was still giving interviews in which he proclaimed his innocence, Camilo came over to eat with us and said that he no longer believed that Cóndor was innocent. By then the rumors were already circulating, but my father and I considered them stupid and defamatory. My father looked at Camilo with contempt, almost with hatred. "You don't have the right to an opinion. You don't know anything about soccer," he told him. "Do you really think Cóndor would be stupid enough to do something like that?" When Rojas finally admitted he was guilty, that he really had hidden a razor blade in his glove to fake an injury, we had no choice but to accept it. We apologized to Camilo then, but he brushed the whole thing off.

For months after watching Cóndor confess, I kept secretly thinking that it couldn't really be possible. But time passed, and eventually we had to stop admiring Cóndor Rojas, and I also stopped going to my father's games. Soon after that my father broke his right hand for the second time, and the doctor told him that he should never play soccer again.

Toward the end of 1990, a marvelous thing happened: after a decade of requesting a telephone line, we finally got one. We were given the number 5573317. The morning they came to install it, I was home alone with my mother. The first thing she did was call one of her girlfriends, and then she told me I should call one of my friends, too, so I called Camilo. It was during a period when he had stopped coming to visit, without explanation. He sounded pleased to hear from me, and I asked him to come see us. He showed up a few days later.

That was the day he wanted to teach me how to talk to girls. I was fourteen by then, I'd already kissed a few girls, but my interactions with them were still clumsy. Camilo said that he'd recently met a girl named Lorena, and they'd gone out on a date and had slept together. He explained how one should treat a woman in bed ("You have to take her clothes off slowly—you can't rush it," I think he said). And now that we had a phone line in the house, he had a proposal: "I'll call Lorena, and you listen in on the phone in your mom's room. That way you'll learn how to seduce a woman," he said. No, Camilo was not showing off—he really did want to teach me.

"Hi, Lorena, it's Camilo," he said in a deep voice.

"Oh, how are you?" Her voice was sweet; sweet, and a little hoarse.

"I'm good, but I need to see you."

She was quiet for five seconds, and then she uttered a sentence that I will never forget. "Well, if it's already a necessity, we'll just end things right here," she said, and hung up.

I went to the kitchen, put the kettle on, and made a cup of tea for Camilo. I think it was the first time I ever made tea for someone. I put a lot of sugar in it, which was what I understood you did when making tea for someone who was sad.

"Thanks," Camilo said with a resigned look. "But it doesn't matter. I'm happy. Next summer something very important is going to happen."

"What?"

"Well, it won't be summer for me. It'll be winter."

It was a perfect clue, but I still didn't understand. How stupid. "I'm going to France to see my father," he said, the excitement clear in his face.

Now I jump ahead many years; twenty-two, to be precise. It's October of 2012. I'm in Amsterdam at a gathering of Chileans, most of them exiles, others students. And there is Big Camilo, Camilo Sr. Someone introduces us, and when he hears my last name I see the interest in his eyes. "You look like your dad," he tells me.

"And you look like Camilo," I reply. He asks me some vague questions. We talk about the protests, about the shameful official refusal to allow Chileans abroad to vote in elections. We talk about Piñera, and suddenly we are compatriots detailing the incompetence of their president. And then: "How is Hernán?" he asks me. "Good," I say, thinking that it's been a while since I've talked to my father. I feel a little bullied, I don't know why. I treat him coldly. Then I realize: Camilo suffered so much because of his father. I feel that, in some dark and absurd way, by talking to Big Camilo I am betraying my friend, my brother. At the same time, I want to talk to this man, to understand who he is. I suggest that we meet up the next day.

We agree to meet at a Mexican restaurant on Keizersgracht. It's a short walk from my hotel. I arrive almost two hours early so I can watch the Barcelona game. Alexis is on the bench. For decades now, soccer has been an individual sport for us Chileans. After what happened with Cóndor Rojas, not only were we out of Italy in '90, we were also forbidden to participate in the South American qualifiers for the '94 World Cup in the United States. We had no choice, for years, but to focus on the local competition and on the individual triumphs and failures of our few countrymen who played outside Chile. We rooted for Real Madrid when Zamorano was there, and now we root for Barcelona, with Alexis Sánchez, for as long as that lasts (if it lasts). And we have been and will be for whatever teams Mati Fernández or Arturo Vidal or Gary Medel or the others play for. We're used to this way of watching: what do goals scored by David Villa and Messi matter to me? The only thing I care about is that they put Alexis in, and, even if he doesn't shine, may he at least not do something dumb.

Big Camilo arrives early, too. I think, I'm going to watch a match with Camilo's dad.

All I know about Big Camilo, about his exile, is what his son told me: that he was imprisoned in 1974, and that he had the good luck, so to speak, to get out of Chile in '75. He went to Paris, and soon met an Argentine woman, with whom he had two children. Now he tells me that he has been in Holland for fifteen years, first in Utrecht, then in Rotterdam, and now in a small town close to Amsterdam. Before long, like a policeman who doesn't want to waste time, I speed up the investigation. I ask why Camilo was so different when he came back to Chile.

"I don't know why," he tells me. "He came to Paris to get me. He wanted us to go back to Chile together. He wasn't interested in moving here, though I asked him to. He told me he was Chilean. I proposed that he come to study. I talked about our plans to settle in Holland. He told me he didn't like studying, not in Santiago and not in Europe. Things got more and more heated. He said horrible things to me. I said horrible things to him. And it became a contest to see who could say the most horrible things. And I ended up feeling that he had won. And he ended up feeling that I had won. All those years we'd kept in touch, I'd thought about him, I'd sent him money—not much, but I sent it. Later, the first time I went back to Chile, we saw each other, we had lunch a few times, but we always fought."

"That was in '92," I say.

"Yes," he replies.

Fifteen minutes into the second half, Alexis goes in; he looks slow, he's offside a couple of times, but he plays a small role in Xavi's 3–0 goal. Then Fábregas scores, and then Messi again. Alexis misses an easy goal in the final minutes.

"What do you think of Alexis?" Big Camilo asks me.

"That he's not better than Messi," I say, and he smiles. I add that he was never much for scoring goals—in Chile he missed goals all the time—but he was an exceptional winger. Suddenly I have that thought again: I'm talking about soccer with Camilo's father, and I feel a kind of tremor. It's a very strange feeling. Though I know Camilo Sr. is a fan of the U, I talk about the 2006 Colo-Colo team. I talk about Claudio Borghi, about Mati Fernández, about Chupete Suazo, Kalule, Arturo Sanhueza. I talk about that terrible finals match against Pachuca at the National Stadium. I feel awkward talking this way. Naive.

Later, I tell him that Camilo wanted him to be my god-father. He smiles as if he doesn't understand. And I don't explain. Then he asks me to use the informal *tú* with him. I say no. He asks if my father and Camilo used the informal with each other. I say yes. "Use it with me, then," he says.

"I'd rather not." I'd like to answer politely, but the only thing that comes out is those weak, murmured words.

I ask him why he and my father had fallen out. My dad never wanted to tell me or Camilo when we asked him: he always changed the subject. And no one else knew. We'd always assumed it was something very serious.

"It was toward the end of the season," Big Camilo tells me. "We had the game all sewn up, two–nil: I was playing center defense, there were only a few minutes left, and your dad was shouting like crazy: 'Pass it, pass it back, pass it, Camilo!' We'd been fighting about that for several games. He never let me make my own decisions. 'Pass it, pass it back!' In those days, the goalie was still allowed to pick the ball up with his hands when you passed it back to him."

"I remember," I tell him. "I'm not that young."

"You are very young," he tells me.

We order more beers.

He goes on, "He kept saying it over and over. 'Pass it back, Camilo, come on!' And I was fed up. Out of pure spite I put the ball in the corner and scored a goal on my own team: "There's your ball, motherfucker!" I told him. Some people laughed, others yelled at me, your father just looked at me with hatred. And then the other team scored, and we tied. If I hadn't scored that own goal, we could have advanced further, maybe even won the championship."

Just then my Dutch friend Luc arrives; he has some books to give me. I introduce him to Camilo. He sits with us for a few minutes, and in his extravagant Spanish he asks Camilo if he's in exile. "Not anymore," Camilo answers. "Or, yes. I don't know anymore." Luc wants me to leave with him, but I feel like I should stay. I tell him we'll meet up later.

Big Camilo had told his son that he was never tortured, even though he was held prisoner for several months. "They beat the shit out of me," he says to me now. "But I don't want to talk about that. I'm alive. I got to leave, start over again." We both fall silent, thinking about Camilo. I remember the record shop, the song by Talking Heads; maybe I hum it a little. "I was born in a house with the television always on . . ."

Now we are walking along Prinsengracht. It's cold. Abstractedly, I start to count the bicycles that are going by at breakneck speed. Fifty, sixty, a hundred. The silence seems definitive. I sense that we're about to say goodbye. And, sure enough, just then he says, "Well, I'll be going now."

"Tell Hernán I'm sorry," he adds. I assure him that my father forgave him years ago, that it's not important. We ask a boy to take our picture with my phone. As we pose, I decide that tomorrow I'm going to call my dad, and we'll talk for a long time about Big Camilo, and we'll also remember, as we do sometimes, the horrendous night in early '94, when Auntie July called to tell us that Camilo had been hit by a car, and the wretched week when he almost pulled through but didn't pull through.

I don't know what makes me ask Big Camilo how he learned of his son's death. "I found out eight days later," he says. "July knew how to contact me, but she didn't." We're standing, staring at the ground, on a corner by a lamp store. I've seen this several times in Amsterdam: shop windows filled with lamps that are all turned on at night. I'm about to tell him this, just to change the subject. Then he repeats, "Please tell Hernán I'm sorry about that own goal."

"I'll tell him," I reply. When we say goodbye, he hugs me and starts to cry. I think that the story can't end like that, with Camilo Sr. crying for his dead son, his son who was practically a stranger to him. But that's how it ends.

Long Distance

I worked nights as a phone operator, and it was one of the best jobs I've ever had. The money wasn't good, but it wasn't awful, either, and although the place looked inhospitable—a cramped office on Guardia Vieja, whose only window looked out on an immense gray wall—it was pleasant to work there, not too cold in winter or too hot in summer. Maybe I did get cold in summer and hot in winter, but that was because I never managed to figure out how to work the thermostat.

This was in 1998: the World Cup in France had ended, and soon after that, when I'd been working at that job for a couple of months, Pinochet was arrested. My boss, who was Spanish, put a photo of Judge Garzón on a corner of the desk, and we placed flowers around it in thanks. Portillo was a good boss, a generous guy. I hardly ever saw him; sometimes we only coincided on the twenty-ninth of the month, when I stuck around until nine a.m., some stupendous circles under my eyes, so I could cash my paycheck. What I remember most about him is his voice, high-pitched like a teenager's—a tone that was common enough among Chileans, but, for me, disconcerting to hear from a Spaniard. He would call me very early, at six or seven in the morning, so I could give him a report on what had happened the previous night, which was pretty much pointless, because nothing ever happened, or almost nothing: maybe a call or two from Rome or Paris, simple cases of people who weren't really sick, but who wanted to make the most of the travel medical insurance they had bought in Santiago. My job was to listen to them, take down their information, make sure the policy was valid, and connect them to my counterparts in Europe.

Portillo let me read or write or even nap on the condition that I always answer the phone in good time. That's why he called at six or seven—although, when he was out partying, he might call earlier, a little drunk. "The phone should never ring more than three times," he would tell me if I took too long picking up. But he didn't usually scold me; on the contrary, he was friendly. Sometimes he asked what I was reading. I would say Paul Celan, or Emily Dickinson, or Emmanuel Bove, or Humberto Díaz Casanueva, and he always burst out laughing, as if he had just heard a very good and unexpected joke.

One night, around four in the morning, I received a call from someone whose voice sounded falsely deep, feigned, and I thought it was my boss pretending to be someone else. "I'm calling from Paris," said the voice. The man was calling direct, which increased my feeling that it was a prank of Portillo's, because clients usually reversed the charges when they called. Portillo and I had a certain level of trust between us, so I told him to quit messing with me, because I was very busy reading. "I don't understand, I'm calling from Paris," the man replied. "Is this the number of the travel insurance?"

I apologized and asked him for his number so I could call him back. When we talked again I had become the nicest phone operator on the planet, which wasn't really necessary, because I've never been impolite, and because the man with the unrealistic voice was also unrealistically nice, which was not the usual in that job: most of the clients shamelessly flaunted their bad manners, their high-handedness, their habit of treating phone operators badly, as they surely also did laborers, cooks, salespeople, and anyone else in the crowded group of supposedly inferior people.

Juan Emilio's voice, on the other hand, suggested the possibility of a reasonable conversation, although I don't know if "reasonable" is the word, because as I was taking down his information (fifty-five years old, home address in Lo Curro, no preexisting conditions) and checking his policy (the best coverage available on the market), something in his voice made me think that, more than a doctor, he needed someone to talk to, someone who would listen.

He told me he'd been in Europe for five months, most of that time in Paris, where his daughter—whom he called la Moño—was working on her doctorate and living with her husband—el Mati—and their kids. None of this was in response to my questions, but he was talking so enthusiastically that it was impossible for me to break in. He told me all about how the kids spoke French with charmingly correct accents, and he also threw in a few banal observations about Paris. By the time he started in about how hard it had been for la Moño to meet her academic obligations, about the complexity of the doctoral programs, and about what kind of sense parenthood made in a world like this one ("a world that sometimes seems so strange these days, so different," he told me), I realized we'd been talking for almost forty minutes. I had to interrupt and respectfully ask him to tell me why he was calling. He said he was a little under the weather, and he'd had a fever. I typed up the fax and sent it to the Paris office so they could coordinate the case, and then I started the long process of saying goodbye to Juan Emilio, who fell all over himself in apologies and courtesies before finally accepting that the conversation had ended.

Around that time I'd picked up a few evening hours teaching at a technical training institute. The schedule fit me perfectly: the class was from 8:00 to 9:20 p.m., twice a week, so I could maintain my nocturnal rhythm, getting up at noon, reading a lot—it was great. My first class was in March 2000, a few days after Pinochet returned to Chile like he owned the place (I'm sorry for these reference points, but they're the ones that come to mind). My students were older than me: they were all at least thirty, and some were in their fifties. They worked all day and struggled to pay their tuition for degree programs in business administration, accounting, secretarial studies, or tourism. I was to teach them "Techniques of Written Expression" according to a very rigid and outdated syllabus, which encompassed composition, grammar, and, oddly, pronunciation.

In the first classes I tried to follow the syllabus as written, but my students came to class very tired from their jobs, and I think all of us got bored. I remember the desolation at the end of those first sessions. I remember that after the third or fourth class I walked down Avenida España and stopped at a hot dog stand, ordered an Italiano, and thought that I should

tackle that feeling of wasted time head-on. After all, I was
there to talk about language, and if there had been one constant in my life it was a love of certain stories, certain phrases,
a handful of words. But it was clear that up to that point I
hadn't been able to communicate anything. "Interesting class,
Prof," one of my students told me at the entrance to the metro,
as if fate were trying to dispel my dark thoughts. I hadn't
recognized her. To combat my shyness, I opted to teach class
without my glasses so I couldn't make out my students' faces.
If I had to ask a question, I'd just look toward some indefinite
place and say, "What do you think, Daniela?" It was an infallible method, because there were five Danielas in the course.

The name of the woman who talked to me in the metro
wasn't Daniela, but it almost rhymed: Pamela. She told me
that she still lived with her parents and didn't have a job. I
asked her why she went to school at night, then. "Because it's
hot during the day," she answered, flirtatious and cavalier. I
asked if she went to school at noon during the winter, and she
laughed. Then I wanted to know if she really thought the class
had been good. She looked down, as if I'd asked her something very personal. "Yes," she told me; then, almost a station
later: "Interesting." We got out together at Baquedano, and I
kept her company while she waited for the bus to Quilicura.

It hadn't been so unusual at university, there'd been tons of
examples: male teacher with student (male or female); female
teacher with student (same); and even a couple salacious cases
(perhaps somewhat exaggerated) of a male teacher with two
female students, and a female teacher with three male students and a female librarian (in the library, on top of the

was the last step before closing a file (oh, what strange pleasure we felt when we finally closed a file). So I picked up the phone and called Paris: Juan Emilio was still at his daughter's house, and it was she who answered. La Moño didn't strike me as quite so friendly as her father: "Call back later," she said dryly. That's what I did. Juan Emilio seemed moved by my call, which tended to happen, because some of the clients thought that we were calling out of personal concern, as if some sad night phone operator would or could ever care about the health of a fellow countryman who travels the world coming down with a slight cold.

Toward the end of the conversation, Juan Emilio asked me if I liked my job. I replied that there were better jobs, but this one was pretty good. "But what did you study?" he insisted. "Literature," I replied, and, inexplicably, he laughed. I hated it when people asked me that, but neither his question nor his laughter bothered me. Over time I learned to accept and appreciate Juan Emilio's crescendos of laughter, minimal at first, and then frank and contagious.

Four or five days later, now back in Chile, he called again. It was seven in the morning, and I was fast asleep in the office. "I wanted to see if you were okay," he told me, and we got caught up in a conversation that would have been normal if we had been two teenagers becoming friends, or two old men trying to combat the inertia of a Monday at their retirement home. I thought Juan Emilio was pretty crazy, and maybe I felt proud to participate in his madness. "Pax very friendly, calls for no reason and thanks me again for the service," I wrote in his file. But really there was a reason for his call, although I think it occurred to him only as we were talking: he asked me to be his teacher, his reading guide. "I need to be more cultured," he said. It seemed simple: I would recommend books for him to read, and then we would discuss them. I accepted, of course. I proposed a monthly sum and he insisted on doubling it. I offered to go to his house or his office, although I didn't really see myself taking the metro and a shared taxi to cross the entire city every week. Luckily, he wanted the classes to take place at my apartment, every Monday, at seven in the evening.

Juan Emilio was short, redheaded, and foppish. He dressed with awkward elegance, as if his clothes were always new, as if his clothes wanted to say, in a loud and forceful voice: I have nothing to do with this body, I will never adapt to this body. We made a reading list that I thought might interest him. He was enthusiastic. I liked Juan Emilio, but the warmth I felt toward him was tempered by an ambiguous, guilty feeling. What kind of person could allow himself such a long European vacation when he was of working age? What had he done all that time, besides take his grandchildren to all the ice cream parlors in Paris? I tried to imagine him as one of those millionaire Chileans who flew to London to support Pinochet. I tried to see him as what I supposed he was: a card-carrying member of the upper crust, conservative, bourgeois, Pinochetista or ex-Pinochetista, though he didn't talk like a typical moneyed Chilean and his opinions weren't so conservative and inflexible: you could talk to him, at least, you really could. Also, Juan Emilio was discreet: he looked around my small apartment on Plaza Italia without revealing that it seemed a poor and run-down place to him. Later, I mollified myself with the reductive thought that no Chilean fat cat would have a daughter studying in France, that France was the worst place in the world for the daughter of a Pinochetista.

The classes at the technical training institute, meanwhile, improved. I started to wear my glasses so I could pay more attention to Pamela. A pair of dimples insinuated themselves into her cheeks, and the way she did her makeup was odd: she drew a thick line around her eyes as if fencing them in, as if she wanted to keep them from jumping out of her skull and escaping. One night we had to go over the various kinds of letter writing, and I rambled on ineloquently until I had the idea to give the class an exercise. I asked them to write a letter that they would have liked to receive, a letter that would have changed their lives. Almost all of them did predictable things, but there were four who took the exercise to extremes and wrote texts that were fierce, devastating, beautiful. One of them ended up crying and cursing his father, or his uncle, or a father who was really his uncle—I think we were all unclear on that point, but we didn't dare ask him to clarify.

I saw that moment as my chance to change course. I devoted the next few classes to lessons on letter writing, trying to help my students discover the power of language, the ability of words to truly influence reality. Some of them were still uneasy, but we started to have a good time. They wrote to their parents, to childhood friends, to first loves. I remember one woman who wrote to John Paul II to explain why she no longer believed in God, and her letter prompted a horrible and convoluted fight that almost came to blows, but in the end we were all better for it. By now they liked the class: the only thing they wanted to do was write letters, express feelings, explore what was happening to them. Except for Pamela, who avoided me and abstained from class participation. And, despite my best efforts, we hadn't run into each other in the metro again.

One night, at the beginning of class, a student raised his hand and told me that he wanted to write a letter of resignation, because he was planning to quit his job. He started talking, then, about the problems he had with his boss; I tried to give him advice, but I was possibly the least qualified person in the room to do that. Someone told him he was irresponsible, that before quitting he should think about how he was going to live and how he would pay for school. A dense, serious silence followed, which I didn't know how to fill.

"I want to write the letter," he told us then. "I'm not going to quit, I couldn't, I have kids, I have problems, but I still want to write that letter. I want to imagine what it would be like to quit. I want to tell my boss how I really feel about him. I want to tell him he's a son of a bitch, but without using that word."

"It's not one word, it's several," said a student sitting in the first row. "What?"

"It's four words: son of a bitch."

We started on the letter. We wrote the first paragraphs on the board, and when the class period was coming to an end, we agreed to continue the exercise next time.

Only there wasn't a next time. I arrived on Monday with just enough time to pick up the course folder and go to the classroom, but the building was locked up and even freshly painted. The institute no longer existed. The students explained all this to me, devastated. They had already paid their tuition for the month, and a few had even paid the whole year in advance, taking advantage of a discount.

That night I went with my students to a bar on Avenida España. They didn't usually go out together and they'd never become friends, so some of them talked about their lives while others focused on their beers and churrasco sandwiches. Pamela was at the opposite end of the table with another group and never talked to me, but I timed things so that, after leaving the bar, we met on the way to the metro. I went with her again to the bus in Plaza Italia, and when we said goodbye she told me that she felt overly watched, but that if I didn't look at her so much, maybe she would start to like me. "But we're never going to see each other again," I told her. "Who knows," she replied.

The sessions with Juan Emilio weren't as easy as I'd thought they'd be. He didn't question the books I chose, but he tried to extract messages and morals from them—as most people do, it must be said. Every week I gave him an exercise to do at home, and he always arrived with a bottle of wine in apology: "I didn't get to finish my homework," he'd tell me with a mischievous look, and then off he would go, talking with dizzying erudition about the vintage or vineyard of the wine he'd brought, using that vocabulary that seemed as funny to me as literary terminology must have seemed to him. Juan Emilio was an executive of something, but I chose not to delve too deeply into his work, basically for the same reason I chose not to ask what he thought about Pinochet's return: I didn't want to find out that he was a bloodsucking plutocrat or something—I didn't want reasons to despise him.

On the other hand, I came to know a lot about his family, and I started to take a real interest in his children's utterly uninteresting lives. As for his marriage, I deduced from our conversations that it was complicated but stable; I'm sure there had been infidelities, but he and his wife were too old by then to separate, and maybe they lived in that world where people didn't separate even if they hated each other. But Juan Emilio didn't hate his wife (who had the terrible but literary name of Eduviges), nor did she hate him. They seemed to tolerate each other, and maybe every once in a while she waited for him with a pisco sour in hand, and they sat down on the sofa to talk about the ill fates of other couples and how good they themselves had it, together and happy after all this time.

It was hard for me to interrupt his speeches and redirect the conversation; in fact, a couple of times it got too late and he had to go before we'd even started the class. He paid me regardless, of course.

I tried to help my ex-students with their complaint before the Ministry of Education, which was offering them little or no recompense. We wrote, among all of us, the Big Letter, the crucial missive that would demonstrate the importance of written communication, the power of words, but nothing happened. We had compiled testimonies, opinions of politicians and experts in education, but to no avail. The situation was scandalous and for a time it was in the news, but then fell that sudden silence, so suspicious and Chilean, which shrouded everything back then. Some of them managed to enroll in other institutes under conditions that were never advantageous, but the ones who had paid for the whole year still didn't have a real solution. And neither did I, I should say: I was owed a month's salary, but when I tried to join forces with the other teachers, I had no luck. I got in touch with two, in fact, who chose not to complain because they also worked at other institutes and they didn't want to get reputations as troublemakers.

Nevertheless, I resolved to see the class through, meeting at that same bar on Avenida España every week. Of the thirty-five original students, ten of them continued with me through the rest of the year, every Wednesday, and although a couple of times things went off the rails, we spent most of those sessions working and discussing. One of those nights, after I had lost all hope, Pamela appeared and joined the group nonchalantly, without comment. We left together for the metro, and she handed me a five-thousand-peso bill. I told her that the class was free, that at most I would let the students pay for my beers and sandwiches during class. She said that she wanted to pay me anyway, and she wouldn't take the money back. "Let's go to your place, Professor," she said to me then, using the formal *usted*. She always used *usted* with me, and I almost don't have to explain how absurd it was for her to do that, since she was ten years older. It was later than usual; I was in the habit of going home and eating a can of tuna before heading to work, but that night I didn't even have time for that. I decided to risk it and bring her to the office. She sucked me off on the rug and then we had sex on Portillo's desk, and luckily the phone didn't ring. At three in the morning we called a taxi, which I charged to the company. Before she left, she told me, with exquisite seriousness: "Pay me, Professor, it's five thousand pesos." It became, after

I couldn't accept his generosity. "This is nothing for me," he replied, which was undoubtedly true, and after refusing two more times, with less conviction, I finally accepted the gifts. Then there was a less than emphatic attempt on my part to begin the class. We vaguely discussed some stories by Onetti while we snacked on cheese and olives and some delicious baklava. I tried, but couldn't hide the fact that I was hungry.

When he was leaving I started to tell him about what we would do the following Monday, but he stopped me. He ran a hand through his hair and lit a cigarette with a speed that was unusual for him, and then said: "I've discovered that I don't really like literature so much. I like to talk to you, to come here, to see how you live. But I haven't really liked anything I've read."

He pronounced these last words with a distasteful emphasis, surely the same tone he used when he fired employees. Something like: "I'm afraid we're going to have to find someone else." Only then did I understand that all that merchandise was a kind of severance pay. Without another word he stood up, looked me straight in the eyes, and leaned in to say goodbye forever with an unexpected and very long kiss on the lips.

I was frozen. It annoyed me that I hadn't understood the plot, and I felt stupid. The kiss didn't offend me, it didn't upset me, but I still took a long drink from a bottle of Syrah; I have no idea if it had a fruity finish or a pronounced acidity, but right at that moment it struck me as fitting.

At work the next night, since it was rumored they were going to cut off the supply again, I collected some water, but

I forgot to turn off the tap. I fell fast asleep on the floor, and I woke up at seven in the morning lying in water, the rug almost entirely drenched. My boss gave free rein to his well-honed sarcasm as he chastised me, but in the end he thought my ineptitude was so funny that he decided not to fire me. I understood, however, that it was the end.

More than once I had thought about staying in that office forever, answering the phone for the rest of my life. It wasn't hard to picture myself at forty or fifty years old, spending the night with my feet up on that same desk, reading the same books over and over. Until then I'd avoided thinking about anything too confusing or elaborate. I never seriously imagined the future, perhaps because I trusted in that thing they call good luck. When I decided to major in literature, for example, all I knew was that I liked to read, and no one could sway me from that. What sort of work I'd do, what kind of life I wanted: I don't know if I ever thought about those things—it would have brought nothing but anxiety. And nevertheless, I guess I wanted to come out ahead, so to speak; I wanted to thrive. The flood was a sign: I needed to succeed in the field I had studied. Or, to be more precise: I needed a job at least slightly connected to what I had studied. I quit right then. At my goodbye dinner, Portillo gave me a book by Arturo Pérez-Reverte, his favorite author.

When I told my students that I was unemployed, they offered to help, although they didn't have any money or contacts or anything. I told them it wasn't necessary, that I had time to look for work, that I had managed to save a bit of money. They looked very serious, but when I told them about the accident at the office, they cracked up, and they agreed that I had to quit. Pamela especially thought so.

We went to my apartment; we could finally sleep together. It was the beginning of October, and the night was pleasant, enticing. We drank an incredible wine, and after sex we watched a quiz show (she got all the questions right) and a movie. We woke up late, but there was no rush. We stayed in bed for an hour while I caressed her generous legs and looked at her feet, perfect but a little diminished by the turquoise polish, now fairly chipped, that she used on her nails. By then we had decided to raise the price: she charged me ten thousand, and I charged her ten thousand.

"You're out of work, but your house is full of food," she said cheerfully as we started thinking about lunch. It really was a lot of food, I thought, and I started to fill a bag with cheeses, cold cuts, cups of yogurt, and bottles of wine. I gave it to her. I was young and much more of a dumbass than I am now, it goes without saying. She listened, stunned, to the stupid sentences I said to her. Only then did I realize I had committed a fatal mistake. Pamela looked at me with rage, in silence, disconcerted, disappointed. She touched one of her breasts, who knows why, as if it hurt her.

Then she picked up the bag and dumped it furiously at my feet. She opened the door and was about to leave without another word, but then she stopped and said, in a broken voice, that she was not and would never be a whore. And that I was not, and would never be, a real professor.

True or False

for Alejandra Costamagna

I got the cat so you would have something here," said Daniel, repeating the psychologist's words exactly, and Lucas showed an enthusiasm that seemed new, unexpected. At his mother's house—"my true house," Lucas called it—there was a little yard where a cat or small dog could have lived happily, but Maru, on that point, was inflexible: no dog, no cat. But from now on, every other week, the boy would get to spend a couple of days with the cat at Daniel's house. They named him Pedro, and later, after they found out it was actually a girl cat, and she was pregnant, they started calling her Pedra.

The "true or false" thing came from school—those were the only exercises that Lucas liked and did well on, and he insisted on applying those categories to everything, capriciously: Maru's house was his true house, but for some reason he judged the living room of that same house to be false— and the armchairs in the living room were true, but the door and all the lamps were false. Only some of his toys were true, but those weren't necessarily the ones he preferred, because falsity didn't imply he disliked something: the few days he spent with his father, for example, at the false house, consisted of a bounteous marathon of Nintendo, pizza, and French fries.

Sometimes Lucas was silent, calm, a bit absent: he seemed to be deep in incommunicable thoughts. But other times he asked questions nonstop, and although he was pretty close to what he was expected to be at nine years old—quite simply, a normal child—his father was unsatisfied and didn't know how to interact with him. Daniel was evidently a normal man, because he had gotten married, had a child, endured several years of family life, and then, as all normal men do, gotten divorced. It was also normal for him to occasionally be late with the alimony payments he owed his ex-wife—almost always out of pure distraction, because he didn't have money problems.

Daniel lived on the eleventh floor of a building where pets were not allowed, but Pedra was discreet: she spent her hours licking her shiny black paws and looking down at the street from the slightly grimy balcony. She didn't need anything more than her bowl of water and a handful of food, which she ate unhurriedly after gazing at the dish for a few minutes, as if deciding whether eating was really worth the trouble. Daniel had never liked cats; he'd lived with a few as a child, but they had really belonged to his brothers. And even so, he was willing to make the effort—a cat is good company, he thought, trusting in an abstract image of a solitary man. Though he wasn't exactly solitary, or he was, but he didn't think solitude was an inconvenience. He'd gotten enough company during the years of his marriage: that's why he left his wife, he thought, out of a need for silence. "I left my wife on grounds of silence," Daniel would say, flirtatiously, if someone were to ask him right now why it had ended, but no one asked him about that anymore, and in any case, that answer wouldn't be true, or false: he needed silence, but he also wanted to save himself, was trying to save himself—or maybe protect himself—from a life he had never wished for.

Maybe he *had* wanted, at some point, to be a father, but it was a fleeting, naive desire. The years they'd lived together ("as a family"), he'd had to be too much of a father. Everything had meaning, every gesture, every sentence held some conclusion or lesson, including his silence—of course, that too. You had to be so cautious with words, so endlessly careful, so depressingly pedagogical: you had to behave like a filter, like a thing, like a dead man. He could be a better father from a distance, he had thought, and that idea was not inspired by any sense of defeat, no, not a hint of it.

His plan had been to tell Lucas that the kittens had died at birth. He was going to drown them without thinking about it much, the way he'd heard it was done: throw them in the toilet, flush, and immediately forget about that bitter secondary scene. But luck was not on his side, and they were born on a day when his son was at his house.

"We can't keep them, Lucas," Daniel told the boy that afternoon.

"Of course we can," replied Lucas. Daniel looked at his son: he thought they looked alike, or they would in the future— their slightly cleft chins, their curly black hair. He helped his son put on the back brace the doctor had prescribed for his scoliosis. Lucas also wore braces on his teeth, and a pair of glasses that made his dark eyes, and even his eyelashes, look bigger.

"Do you have homework?" Daniel asked.

"Yeah."

"Do you want to do it?"

"No."

What they did instead was make phone calls offering the kittens up for adoption and draft an email that Daniel sent out to all his contacts. When he dropped Lucas off at his true house, Daniel got mired in a bitter argument with his ex-wife, in which he tried to convince her that she was the one who should take on the responsibility of the kittens.

"Sometimes I forget what you're like," Maru said to him.

"And what am I like?"

Maru didn't answer.

During the following weeks, the cats opened their eyes and started to crawl laboriously around the living room. There were five of them: two black, two gray, and one that was almost entirely white. To avoid repeating the mistake of Pedro/Pedra, Lucas decided not to name them. Now that there were kittens at his father's house, Lucas wanted to be there all the time. For Daniel it was a triumph, but an uncomfortable one.

At seven in the evening one Thursday, Lucas showed up at Daniel's out of nowhere. Five minutes later Maru appeared, panting after climbing the eleven flights of stairs to his apartment. She hated elevators, hated that Daniel lived on the eleventh floor—and not only because she was concerned for her son's safety, or because of her own phobia, but because she still remembered, persistently, that long-ago night when Daniel had promised that there would be no elevators, that they would always live, so to speak, with their feet on the ground.

Maru apologized for the visit by saying they'd been in the neighborhood, which was highly unlikely since they lived on the other side of the city.

"For a second I thought Lucas came alone," said Daniel.

"What do you mean, alone?"

"Alone."

"Are you crazy?"

"No."

Daniel toasted some bread and made coffee, which they drank in silence while the boy assigned nationalities to the cats: the white or almost-white cat was Argentine, the black cats were Brazilian, and the gray cats were Chilean.

Thanks to the group emails, Daniel got back in touch with an ex-classmate from college, a woman who came over one night on the pretense of adopting a cat. After the first pisco and Coke they went to bed, and it was good, or more or less good, as she said the next morning.

"I mean, I liked it," she added lightly, but to Daniel it seemed like an aggressive remark. "What happened to you is really strange," she said next; she had the habit of changing the subject every time she lit a cigarette: "it's really strange what happened to you—it's more common for male cats to be mistaken for female, and not the other way around."

"What?"

"Just, it's normal to not see their cocks well. But you saw a cock on Pedra where there wasn't one," said the woman, who hardly had time to laugh at her joke before she told another one: "She's called Pedra and you're called *Padre*."

Daniel laughed late, irritated.

"Why do you call it a 'cock'?" he asked her.

"Why shouldn't I?"

"Women don't say 'cock.'"

"But what you put in me last night is called a 'cock,'" she said. "And what Pedra doesn't have is called a 'cock.'"

To Daniel it seemed like phony indecency. Before leaving, the woman assured him that she would come by later for the cat, and, in a fit of optimism, Daniel imagined that the scene from the night before would repeat over and over: every evening, his friend would come for a cat, sleep with him, and leave at dawn. But it wasn't like that, not at all. She never came back, didn't call, didn't write.

A rumor spread that there were cats in the building, so Daniel had to bribe the concierges with a bottle of pisco and a few opportune boxes of Gato Negro wine, as a joke. Then it took several whiskeys to neutralize the next-door neighbors, a Catalan playwright and his wife.

"We like the country, and the neighborhood is very clean," they said almost in unison, as if they were in a contest that measured matrimonial harmony. Pedra sniffed at the guests while the kittens dozed in a pile inside a shoebox. The couple had come to Chile to be near their daughter, who'd just had a baby. The woman spent a lot of time with the granddaughter, and the man tended to stay home alone—he was in need of a little solitude and inspiration, he explained.

Solitude and inspiration, Daniel thought later as he lay in

bed. He had solitude and he'd never needed inspiration, but when he heard the playwright's words, he thought maybe that was, precisely, what he was missing: inspiration. His job, however, was very simple, almost mechanical: a lawyer doesn't need inspiration, but rather the patience to tolerate his superiors, and surely also the intelligence and subtlety to undermine and supplant them, and maybe also imagination, but only practical imagination, he told himself, as though definitively solving a great conundrum.

I only look for inspiration when I jack off, he thought later, wide awake, evoking the happiness of a table full of good friends who would celebrate that sentence, and then he started to masturbate, taking inspiration first from the playwright's wife, especially her legs, and then from that friend of his who never came back, and finally from Maru, who was still attractive to him, although the image he focused on was one from their youth, from those first years when they sometimes had sex in motels, and especially from a trip home on Route 78, when he drove some twenty kilometers with her bent over, sucking him off. He focused on that memory and proceeded hurriedly, uneasily, greedily, but the semen wouldn't come—he didn't come. It was hard to convince himself that he just had to go to sleep, erection and all, still half drunk.

The next day he was supposed to pick Lucas up, but he overslept and called Maru with the lie that he had a headache. She put Lucas on the phone and Daniel promised to pick him up at five—"We can make sushi, I learned how," he said, which was a lie, but Daniel liked to casually toss out that kind of lie, to force himself to transform it into truth.

After ten minutes online he knew what he needed to buy at the store. In addition to the sushi supplies, he returned home with a large bag of Whiskas, a lot of milk, and bottles of Bilz, Pap, and Kem Piña, because he could never manage to remember which soda was his son's favorite.

"These cats need a dad," Lucas said that night as he fought with a disastrous sushi roll.

"Cats don't have dads," Daniel answered hesitantly. "When they're in heat, the girl cats have sex with whoever, and the kittens aren't always even real brothers and sisters."

"What?"

"Just that—they're not necessarily real siblings. They're half siblings, that's why they're different colors. Most likely Pedra had sex with three boy cats: one gray, one white, and one that was black, like her."

"I don't care," said Lucas, who seemed to have thought about the matter beforehand. "I don't care. I think that these cats definitely need a dad."

"We already have a lot of cats, Lucas, and also, cats are different from humans. The dad cats forget about their babies," said Daniel, for a second fearing an acidic answer that didn't come. "And the moms do, too," he went on cautiously. "After a while, it's likely that Pedra won't recognize her babies."

"I don't believe you," said the boy, astonished. "That's impossible."

"You'll see. Now she worries about them, carries them around in her mouth, gathers them together, cries if she can't find them. But soon she'll forget about them. That's how animals are."

"You sure know a lot about animals," said Lucas, and Daniel couldn't tell if his tone was ironic or earnest.

"Not really, but your uncles had cats."

"But you lived in the same house."

"Sure, but the cats weren't mine."

They were in the bedroom, watching a very slow Mexican soccer match, about to fall asleep. Daniel went to the kitchen to get a glass of water and stood there for a few minutes watching Pedra, who seemed either committed or resigned to the kittens' scrabbling at her teats. He went back to the bedroom; Lucas had closed his eyes and was murmuring a kind of litany—Daniel thought he was having a nightmare and shook him lightly, trying to wake him up.

"I wasn't sleeping, Dad, I was praying."

"Praying? Since when do you pray?"

"Since Monday. On Monday I learned how to pray."

"Who taught you?"

"Mom."

"Since when does she pray?"

"She doesn't. But she taught me to pray, and I like it."

They slept, as always, in the same bed. That night there was a small earthquake and hundreds of dogs howled pitifully, but Daniel and Lucas didn't wake up. That night, there was the far-off thunder of a car crash, as well as the nearby voices of the neighbors, who were arguing or talking or maybe rehearsing a scene in which two people argued or talked. But Lucas and Daniel slept well, breakfasted better, and spent the morning playing Double Dragon.

"I'm sure that Pedra's babies are true," Lucas told his father later, at the park.

"Without a doubt they are true, they're completely true, you can be sure of that. A friend of mine told me recently that our confusion about Pedra was strange. According to my friend, normally people think boy cats are girls, not that girl cats are boys."

"I don't understand," said the child.

"I don't really understand, either. It's complicated. Forget it."

"Forget about your friend?"

"Yes, my friend," said Daniel, annoyed.

Daniel invited the Catalans over for coffee.

"You all have a wonderful country," said the playwright's wife, looking at Lucas.

"Lucas thinks Santiago is false," Daniel told his guests.

"No!" shouted the boy. "Chile is false, Santiago is true."

"What about Barcelona?" they asked. Lucas shrugged his shoulders and started to play with some papers on the floor, as though he were one of the cats. He was wearing shorts, and his legs were covered in scratches, as were his arms and right cheek.

"The situation in Chile is incredible," said the playwright with either a reflective or a questioning tone. "Doesn't it bother you that Pinochet still has so much power? Aren't people afraid that the dictatorship will come back?"

"Weren't you just talking about how peaceful Chile is?" Daniel answered.

"That's precisely what bothers me about the situation here," said the playwright, sententiously: "Everything is so calm, so civilized." Then he strung together a speech featuring words that reminded Daniel of papers he had to read once upon a time, at university, in tedious elective courses: globalization, postmodernity, hegemony.

"I voted for Aylwin and for Frei," was Daniel's only response, revealing just how lost he was. When his guests finally left, he asked Lucas if the Catalans were true or false.

"They were weird," Lucas replied.

That afternoon they lost the white kitten, the Argentine. Daniel, Lucas, and Pedra looked everywhere for it, but it never turned up. There was no way it could have jumped or gotten out, so during the following weeks Daniel had to move around the house with extreme caution. When he got home from work, he went stealthily through the rooms, always barefoot, practically on tiptoe, and he took extra care anytime he sat or lay down. One morning, almost a month after it disappeared, he saw the white kitten sleeping peacefully next to its mother. It had returned from who knew where and taken its place with a nonchalance that irritated Daniel. Over the phone, his son was happy with the news, but there was no euphoric shouting like Daniel had expected.

"Why are you talking so quietly?" he asked.

"I don't want to wake them up," replied Lucas, still whispering.

"Who?"

"The cats."

"The cats aren't sleeping," said Daniel, with a touch of rage. "So you can just talk normally, okay?"

"Don't lie to me, Dad, I know they're sleeping."

"It's not true. And even if they were sleeping, and you shouted over the phone, you wouldn't wake them up. You know that."

"Yeah, I know. I have to go."

"Is something wrong?"

It was the first time his son had ever hung up on him. He called Maru's cell phone, and she was polite, much nicer than usual. Nothing strange was going on, then, thought Daniel, resigned, in the middle of the conversation. But suddenly, as though she'd just been struck by a casual thought, Maru said that maybe it would be better for the cats to live with her.

"But you don't like cats. You have a phobia."

"No, I don't have a phobia. I have a phobia with elevators, spiders, and pigeons. What's that called?"

"What?"

"The fear of pigeons."

"Colombophobia," replied Daniel, exasperated. "Stop asking stupid questions and tell me why you want the cats. You've never let Lucas have one before."

"It's just that he talks about them a lot. I'd like for them live with us. And we can give them away gradually, and keep only Pedra. I already talked to some girlfriends who would love to have a cat."

Maru and Daniel fought like never before, or rather exactly like before. An inexplicable rhetorical twist had reversed things: not even the best lawyer in the world—and Daniel was certainly not the best lawyer in the world—could convince Maru that it was not her right to decide the fate of the cats. The negotiation was long and erratic, since Daniel wasn't necessarily against the idea, but he hated to lose. He didn't want them, really, except maybe Pedra—he did everything in his power to keep Pedra. At least ten times he said, "You can have the babies, but Pedra does not leave this house," and all ten times, he had to endure reasonable and dangerous arguments about a mother's rights.

"You can have the white one then, if you want her," said Maru, finally.

"We don't know if it's a boy or a girl," said Daniel, for the sheer pleasure of correcting her.

"Lucas thinks it's a girl," she replied. "But fine, that's not the point. Do you or do you not want the white cat, boy or girl?"

He said he did. The day they moved the cats into the true house, Lucas was happy.

Daniel still hasn't decided what to name the white cat. He calls it Argentina or Argentino indiscriminately. When he flops into the armchair to read the paper, the cat comes to sit between the page and his eyes, kneading at his sweater, intensely concentrated.

"I've had to get used to reading standing up," he says to his neighbors, glass in hand. They have come over to say good-bye, because they're returning to Barcelona soon.

"It must have been hard for you to lose the kittens," says the playwright.

"Not too bad," replies Daniel. "It must be harder to write plays," he adds obligingly, then asks why they have to go, since he seemed to remember that they'd planned to leave the following year. The question, for some reason, is inappropriate, and the playwright and his wife stare at the floor, maybe at the same point on the floor.

"It's personal. Family problems," says the woman.

"And were you able to write?" asks Daniel, to change the subject.

"Not much," she says, as if she were in charge of answering all the questions. The scene strikes Daniel as grotesque, or at least embarrassing—above all because of that slippery expression, "family problems." He had been in a good mood, but suddenly he is lost, or bored. He wants them to leave soon.

"So what did you want to write about?" he asks, without the slightest interest.

"He doesn't know. He doesn't know what it's about," she says. "Maybe the transition."

"What transition?"

"Chile's, Spain's. Both, in comparison."

Daniel quickly imagines one or two boring plays, with actors who are very old or too young, bellowing like they are at the market. Then he asks how many pages the playwright has written in Santiago.

"Fifty, seventy pages, but none of it works," answers the woman.

"And how do you know that none of it works?"

"I don't know, ask him."

"I am asking him. All of these questions have been for him. I don't know why you answered."

The playwright is still aggrieved. The woman is caressing his hair. She whispers something to him in Catalan, and right away, without looking at Daniel, they leave the apartment. They are sad and offended, but Daniel doesn't care. For some reason, he feels furious. He drinks whiskey until dawn; from time to time the Argentine cat jumps up, com-

passionately, onto his lap. He thinks of his son. He feels
like calling him, but doesn't. He thinks about saving money
to buy a house on the beach. He thinks about changing something, anything: paint some walls, buy a few grams of coke,
let his beard grow out, improve his English, learn martial
arts. Suddenly he looks at the cat and finds a name for it—a
perfect, androgynous name—but immediately, in his drunk-
enness, he forgets it. How is it possible to forget a name so
quickly? he thinks. And then he doesn't think anything anymore, because he drops onto the carpet and doesn't wake up
until the following afternoon. He finds, as his hangover blos-
soms, that he has missed work, that he hasn't heard his phone
ring some ten or fifteen times, that he's left many emails un-
read. The cat is sleeping beside him, purring. Daniel tries to
see if it has a penis or not. "Nothing," he says out loud. "You
don't have a cock. You're a girl cat," he tells it, solemnly.
"You are a true girl cat."

He gets up, prepares an Alka-Seltzer, and drinks it without waiting for the tablet to dissolve entirely. His head hurts,
but he still puts on an album he's discovered recently, a selec-
tion of old waltzes, tangos, and foxtrots that remind him of
his grandfather. While he showers, the cat chases his shadow
on the shower curtain. He sings along with a silly song in a
low voice, more sad than happy. Then he lies down on the
bed for a few minutes, as he always does, still wet and with
the towel around his waist. The phone rings: it's the playwright, who wants to apologize for the night before by inviting him to dine.

"In Chile we don't 'dine,' in Chile we 'eat,'" he answers.
"And I don't want to dine or eat. I want to jerk off," he says,
forcing an imperfectly crude tone.

Memories of a
Personal Computer

I t was bought on March 15, 2000, for 400,080 pesos, payable in thirty-six monthly installments. Max tried to fit the three boxes into the trunk of a taxi, but there wasn't enough room, so he had to use string and a bungee cord to secure everything, though it was only a short ten-block trip to Plaza Italia. Once in the apartment, Max installed the heavy CPU as best he could under the dining room table, arranged the cables in a more or less harmonious way, and played like a kid with the bubblewrap it had been packaged in. Before solemnly starting up the system, he took a moment to look at everything deliberately, fascinated: the keyboard seemed impeccable, the monitor, perfect, and even the mouse and speakers had a certain charm.

At twenty-three years old he had never owned a computer before, and he didn't know exactly what he wanted it for, considering he barely knew how to turn it on and open the word processor. But it was necessary to have a computer, everyone said so, even his mother, who'd promised to help him with the payments. He worked as an assistant at the university and he thought that maybe he could type up the reading tests or transcribe his old notes, written by hand or laboriously typed on an old Olympia typewriter, on which he had also written all his undergraduate papers, provoking the laughter or admiration of his classmates, who were, by then, all using computers.

The first thing he did was transcribe the poems he had written over the past several years—short texts, elliptical and incidental, which were considered good by no one, but they weren't so bad, either. Something happened, though, when he saw those words on the screen, words that had made so much sense in his notebooks: he began to doubt the verses, and to get swept up in a different rhythm—maybe one that was more visual than musical. But instead of feeling like the change of style was an experiment, he pulled back, got frustrated, and very often just deleted the poems and started over again, or wasted time changing fonts or moving the mouse pointer from one side of the screen to the other, in straight lines, in diagonals, in circles. He still didn't renounce his notebooks or his fountain pen, and at the first slipup he splattered ink all over the keyboard, which also had to endure the threatening presence of countless cups of coffee and a continual rain of ash, because Max almost never made it to the ashtray, and he smoked a lot while he wrote, or rather, he wrote a little while he smoked a lot. Years later the accumulated grime would lead to the loss of the vowel *a* and the consonant *t*, but that's getting ahead of things, and it would be best, for now, to respect the proper sequence of events.

The computer inaugurated a new kind of solitude. Max didn't watch the news anymore, or while away time playing the guitar or drawing; when he came back from the university he would immediately turn on the computer and start working or exploring the machine's possibilities. Soon he discovered very simple programs whose capabilities struck him as astonishing, such as the voice recorder, which he used with a puny little microphone that he bought at Casa Royal, or the "shuffle" playback option—he looked proudly at his My Music folder, which now hosted all twenty-four of the compact discs he owned. While he listened to those songs, amazed at how a ballad by Roberto Carlos could segue into the Sex Pistols, he continued working on his poems, which he never considered finished. Sometimes, lacking a heater, Max fought off the cold by kneeling down and embracing the CPU, whose low hum merged with the refrigerator's snore and the voices and horns that filtered in from outside. He wasn't interested in the internet, he distrusted it, and though at his mom's house a friend had set him up with an email account, he refused to connect his computer to the internet, or to insert those diskettes that were so dangerous: potential virus carriers, he'd been told, with the power to ruin everything.

The few women who came to his apartment during those months all left before dawn, without even showering or eating breakfast, and they didn't come back. But at the beginning of summer there was one who did stay to sleep, and then also stayed for breakfast: Claudia. And she came back—once, twice, many times. One morning, emerging from the shower, Claudia stopped in front of the darkened screen as if looking at her reflection, searching for incipient wrinkles or some other stray mark or blemish. Her face was dark, her lips more thin than full, her neck long, her eyes dark green and almond-shaped, and her hair hung down to her wet shoulders: the tips were like needles stuck into her bones. The towel that she herself had brought over to Max's house could wrap around her body twice. Weeks later, Claudia also brought over a mirror for the bathroom, but she still went on looking at herself in the screen, though it was difficult to find, in the darkness of her reflection, anything more than the outline of her face.

After sex, Max tended to fall asleep, but Claudia would go to the computer and play quick games of solitaire, or cautious ones of minesweeper, or intermediate ones of chess. Sometimes he would wake up and go sit next to her, giving her advice on the game or caressing her hair and back. Claudia gripped the mouse tightly in her right hand like someone was going to snatch it from her, and she clenched her teeth and widened her eyes exaggeratedly, but every once in a while she let out a nervous giggle that seemed to give him permission to go on caressing her. Maybe she played better with him beside her. When the game ended she'd sit on Max's lap and they would begin a long, slow screw. The strange lights of the screen saver drew fickle lines on her shoulders, on her back, her buttocks, on Claudia's soft thighs.

They drank coffee in bed, but sometimes they made space at the table so they could sit down to eat breakfast "the way God intended," as she would say. Max would unplug the keyboard and monitor and set them on the floor, exposing them to treading feet and minuscule breadcrumbs, and so, every once in a while, Claudia used glass cleaner and a kitchen rag to wipe them down. But the computer's conduct, during this period, was exemplary: Windows always started up successfully.

On the thirtieth of December, 2001, almost two years after its purchase, the computer moved neighborhoods to a
slightly larger apartment in Ñuñoa. Its surroundings were
significantly more favorable now: it had its own room and
its own desk, which had been assembled from an old door
and two sawhorses. Claudia graduated from hands of solitaire and interminable chess games to more sophisticated
activities—she connected a digital camera, for instance, that
contained dozens of photos from a recent trip, which, though
it couldn't exactly be considered a honeymoon, because Max
and Claudia weren't married, had more or less functioned as
one. The images showed her posing with the ocean behind
her, or in a wood-paneled room with Mexican sombreros and
immense crucifixes on the walls, and shells that served as
ashtrays. She was serious or holding back laugher, naked or
wearing very little, smoking weed, drinking, covering her
breasts or displaying them mischievously. ("Your lustful,
wanton face that calls to me," he wrote on an afternoon that
was certainly hot but maybe a little too iambic-pentametered.)
There were also some photos that showed only the rocks or
the waves or the sun going down on the horizon, a series of
imitation postcards. Max appeared in only two photos, and
only one showed both of them, embracing, smiling, a typical
seaside restaurant in the background. Claudia spent days organizing those images: she renamed the files with phrases
that were too long and tended to end in exclamation points or
ellipses, and she grouped the files into several folders, as if
they corresponded to many different trips, but then she put
them all together again, thinking that, in a few years, there

would be many more files—fifty, a hundred folders for all the photos from a hundred future trips, because she wanted a life full of travel and photographs. She also spent hours trying to beat level 5 on a Pink Panther game that came as a free gift with the detergent. When she despaired, Max tried to help her, though he had always been terrible at video games. They were so tense and concentrated as they looked at the screen, you would have thought they were solving arduous and urgent problems on which the future of the country or world depended.

Their schedules didn't always coincide in the new house, because now Max had a night job—he had lost the contest for assistantships at the university, or rather the professor's new girlfriend had won—and Claudia sold insurance and was also studying for some kind of postgraduate certificate. Sometimes they would go one or two days without seeing each other—Claudia would call him at work and they would talk for a long time, since Max's job consisted, precisely, of talking on the phone, or waiting for remote telephone calls that never came. "Seems like your real job is talking to me on the phone," Claudia told him one night, the receiver sliding off her right shoulder. Then she laughed with a kind of wheeze, as if she had to cough but the cough wouldn't come, or it had gotten mixed up with the laugh.

Like Max, Claudia preferred to write by hand and then transfer her work to the computer. The documents she wrote were very long and featured childish fonts and frequent transcription errors. They dealt with matters related to cultural administration or politics or native forests, etc. It became necessary for her to do research on the internet, and this was a big change, which led to the couple's first fight, because Max still refused to use the internet—he wanted nothing to do with web pages or antiviruses, but in the end, he had to give in. Then, one night, there was a second furious argument: Max had been calling insistently for hours, but he couldn't get through because Claudia was online. They bought a cell phone to solve the problem, but it was too expensive for their long conversations, and they had to get a second landline.

Before then, neither of them had really spent much time on email, but soon, they both became addicts; Max's greatest newfound addiction, however—one he would never kick—was pornography. This led to the couple's third big argument, but also to several experiments, like the disconcerting—to Claudia, at least—ejaculations on her face, and Max's obsession with anal sex, which provoked irate but ultimately beneficial discussions about the possible limits of pleasure.

It was around then that they lost the vowel *a* and the consonant *t*. It happened on a night when Claudia was urgently trying to finish a report, so she tried to make do without those letters. Max, who once upon a time had attempted to write experimental poems, tried to help her, but to no avail. The next day they bought a very good keyboard: it was black and had some coy pink multimedia buttons that allowed you to play or stop the music instantaneously, without having to resort to the mouse.

For some months, however, there had been portents of a greater disaster: dozens of inexplicable delays, some of them short and reversible, others so long they had to give in and restart the computer. It finally happened one rainy Saturday, which they should have spent cozily watching TV and eating sopaipillas, or, in the worst of cases, moving the cooking pots and basins from one leaky spot to another. Instead they had to devote the whole day to repairing the computer—or trying to repair it, more by force of will than any real, coordinated strategy.

On Sunday, Max called in a friend who was studying engineering. By the end of the afternoon, two bottles of pisco and five cans of Coca-Cola dominated the desk, but no one was drunk, they were just frustrated by the difficulty of the repair job, which Max's friend attributed to "something very strange, something I've never seen before." But maybe they really were drunk, or at least Max's friend was, because all of a sudden, in one disastrous maneuver, he erased the hard drive. "Well, you lost everything, but from now on it will work better," said the friend nonchalantly, his coldness and fortitude worthy of a doctor who had just amputated a leg.

"It was your fault, you asshole," said Claudia, sounding as if one or maybe both of her legs really had been cut off out of pure negligence. Max kept quiet and hugged her protectively. The friend took one final and exaggerated gulp of his pisco and Coke, grabbed a few cubes of gouda for the road, and left.

Claudia had a hard time absorbing the loss, but she called in a real technician, who changed the operating system and created separate profiles for both users, and even a symbolic third account, at Claudia's request, for Sebastián, Max's son. Yes, it's true, he should have come up sooner, over two thousand words had to go by before he came into play, but the thing is that Max often forgot about the child's existence: in recent years he'd seen him just once, and only for two days. Claudia had never even met him, because Sebastián lived in Temuco. It was hard for her to understand the situation, which had become, naturally, the black spot or blind spot in her relationship with Max. It was better not to broach the subject, though it still came up every once in a while, in vicious arguments that ended with both of them in tears, and of the two, it was he who cried the most—he sobbed with rage, with resentment, with shame, and then his face would harden as though the tears had settled like sediment onto his skin; it's a commonplace analogy, but after he'd been crying, his skin really did look denser and darker.

It wasn't all so terrible. When Claudia used some money from her parents to buy an amazing all-in-one device—it could print, scan, and even make photocopies—she threw herself passionately into digitizing extensive family albums. She would sit in front of the computer for hours, and although those sessions seemed fairly tedious, she enjoyed them because she wasn't just documenting the past, she was altering it: she distorted the faces of her more obnoxious relatives, she erased secondary characters and added in other, more unlikely guests, like Jim Jarmusch (at her birthday party), or Leonard Cohen (beside young Claudia taking her first communion), or Sinéad O'Connor, Carlos Cabezas, and the congressman Fulvio Rossi (tagging along on a trip to San Pedro de Atacama). The editing wasn't very good, but it got some laughs out of friends and cousins.

And so another year passed.

Now Max worked the morning shift, so in theory they had more time together, but they wasted a good portion of that time arguing over the computer. He complained that because Claudia was on it so much he wasn't able to write when inspiration struck, which was untrue, because he still used the same old notebooks for his endless drafts of poems (he felt that they were destroyed by the process of transcription). He had gotten into the habit of writing endless emails to people he hadn't seen in years, whom he now missed, or thought he missed. Some of these people lived nearby or not so far away, and Max also had their phone numbers, but he preferred to write them letters—they were letters more than emails: melancholic, sensationalist, and wistful, the kind of messages whose replies are put off indefinitely, although sometimes he received responses that were every bit as elaborate and equally contaminated by a frivolous, whining nostalgia.

Summer arrived, and so did Sebastián, after months of delicate negotiations. They both went to Temuco to pick him up, by bus, nine hours there and almost ten back. The boy had just turned eight years old, and the slight, premature shadow of a mustache gave him a comical, grown-up look. During his first days with them, Sebastián spoke little, especially if he was answering his father. The intense trips to downtown Santiago, the zoo, and Fantasilandia gave way to sweltering afternoons spent at home, and it's possible they had a better time shut away indoors than during all those supposedly fun activities. Seba took advantage of his user profile, signing into Messenger without restrictions for interminable chats with his Temucan friends. He quickly demonstrated a knowledge of computers, which wasn't surprising—like most children of his generation, he had learned about them from a young age—but the extent of his dexterity impressed Claudia and Max. In a precise, slightly bored tone, the boy educated them about their options for a new antivirus and explained how they needed to defrag the hard drive periodically. He ran through the Pink Panther game with astonishing speed, it goes without saying, and the two or three afternoons he spent teaching his father and Claudia the logic of the game— so elementary for him—were the most glorious and full moments of that vacation. He had certainly never been so close to his father, and he and Claudia became friends, as it were. Claudia thought Sebastián was a good kid, and Sebastián thought Claudia was pretty.

They all went back to Temuco together. The trip was a happy one, with gifts and promises of future visits. But the bus ride home was somber and exhausting, a distinct prelude to what was coming next. Because, the moment they opened the door to the apartment, life entered into an irresolvable paralysis. Maybe annoyed by Claudia's conclusions and advice ("You got him back, but now you have to keep him," "You'll lose him again if you don't take care of your relationship," "Seba's mother is a good woman") or maybe just bored with her, Max withdrew, sank into himself. He didn't hide his annoyance, but wouldn't explain his mood, either, and he ignored Claudia's endless questions, or else answered them in reluctant monosyllables.

———

One night he came home drunk and went to sleep without even greeting her. She didn't know what to do. She went to bed, embraced him, tried to sleep next to him, but she couldn't. She turned on the computer, idly surfed the internet, and spent two hours playing Pac-Man with the arrow keys. Then she called a taxi and went to a liquor store to buy white wine and menthol cigarettes. She drank half the bottle at the table in the living room, looking at the cracks in the laminate flooring, the white walls, the faint but numerous fingerprints on the light switches—from my fingers, she thought, plus Max's, plus the fingers of all the people who ever turned on the lights in this apartment. Then she went back to the computer, clicked on Max's profile, and as she had done many times before, tried the obvious passwords, in capital letters, in lowercase—*charlesbaudelaire, nicanorparra, anthrax, losprisioneros, starwars, sigridalegria, blancalewin, mataderocinco, laetitiacasta, juancarlosonetti, monicabellucci, confederacyofdunces.* She apprehensively smoked a cigarette, five cigarettes, while she tuned into a new anxiety, one that grew and shrank at an imprecise rhythm. She overthought an option that was also obvious, but that out of modesty or low self-esteem she had never tried: she typed in *claudiatoro* and the system responded immediately. The email program was open and didn't require a password. She stopped, poured more wine, was about to desist, but she was already there, facing the formidable inbox and the even more formidable record of sent messages. There was no turning back.

She read, in no particular order, messages that were ultimately innocent, but hurt her nonetheless—so many times the word "dearest," so many hugs ("a big hug," "xoxo," and other, perhaps more original formulations, like "sending hugs," "hugging you," "sending hugs your way"), so many references to the past, and that suspicious ambiguity when he had to write about the present or the future. There were the kind of fleeting, fierce flirtations that show up in everyone's email accounts, hers too, but there were also five chains of messages that spoke of meetings with women she didn't know. But what hurt the most was her own invisibility, because he never mentioned her, at least not in the messages she read—except for one, sent to a friend, in which he confessed that the relationship was on the rocks: he literally wrote that he wasn't interested in sex with her anymore, and that they would probably break up any day now.

She closed the email and went to sleep at dawn, intoxicated with rage more than wine. She woke up in the mid-afternoon, alone. Listlessly, she walked to the computer—just to the room next door, though to her it seemed like a long journey—but instead of turning it on, she stared at the glare of the sun on the monitor. She closed the blinds, wishing for absolute darkness, while tears flowed down her neck and disappeared in the furrow between her breasts. She sat down on the floor and took off her shirt, looked at her alert nipples, her smooth, soft belly, her knees, her fingers firm on the cold floor. Then she got up and wiped the screen clean, or rather, dirtied it with her fingers that were wet with tears. She moved her fingers and knuckles angrily over the surface, as if scrubbing it with a rag. Then she turned on the computer, wrote a short note in Word, and started packing her suitcase.

She came back the next Sunday to pick up some books and the all-in-one device.

Max was in his underwear at the computer, writing a long email to Claudia in which he talked about a thousand things, and in which he apologized, but in an elliptical way, with sentences that left his confusion, or mediocrity, in plain view. There were other drafts of the letter on the desk, seven or eight sheets of legal-size paper, and while he protested that it wasn't fair—he hadn't gotten to finish his letter, it was full of mistakes, he had trouble saying things clearly—Claudia read the different versions of that unsent message, and she noticed how a definitive phrase in one draft became ambiguous in the next, how he changed adjectives, cut and pasted phrases. And she noticed, too, how he had adjusted the line and character spacing, the font size, and it was these changes in particular that struck Claudia as sordid—it was like he thought she would forgive him if the message seemed longer, and that's what she was thinking about when he grabbed her and held her by the wrists, knowing that she hated to be held by the wrists, and as they were struggling he hit her in the breasts, and she responded with four slaps, but he won out and bent her over and forced himself into her, penetrating her ass with a violence he'd never shown before. She grabbed the keyboard and tried to defend herself, unsuccessfully. Two minutes later, Max ejaculated a meager amount of semen, and she turned around and stared at him, as if suggesting a truce, but instead of embracing him she kneed him in the balls. While Max writhed in pain, she unhooked the all-in-one device and called a taxi that would take her far away from that house forever.

Max felt an immense but short-lived relief. Her relief was hard-won and took its time in coming, but once it did, it came to stay. And so, three months later, when she reluctantly agreed to meet him on the steps of the National Library and he begged her, without the slightest sense of decorum, to come back, she was almost able to laugh in his face.

He went home sad and furious, and out of habit turned on the computer, which had been crashing a lot recently; for some reason, when it crashed this time, Max decided it was finished.

"I'm going to give it away, I don't care about anything stored on it," he said the next day to his engineer friend, who offered to buy it for a ridiculously small amount.

"Hell no," said Max. "I'm going to give it to my son."

"Fine," the friend said, and he reluctantly wiped the hard drive clean.

That Friday, Max took an overnight bus to Temuco. He had no time to box up the computer, so he put the mouse and the microphone in his pockets, the CPU and keyboard under the seat, and he rode all nine hours with the heavy screen on his lap. The lights on the highway shone onto his face, as though calling him, inviting him, as though blaming him for something, for everything.

Max didn't know his way around Temuco, and he hadn't

written down the address. He hailed a taxi at the bus stop, and they drove around for a long time before coming to a street that Max thought he recognized. He arrived at ten in the morning, zombified. When he saw Max, Sebastián immediately asked about Claudia, as if the surprise were not his father's unexpected presence but the absence of his father's girlfriend. "She couldn't come," answered Max, going for a hug he didn't know how to give.

"Did you break up?"

"No, we didn't break up. She just couldn't come, is all. Grown-ups have to work."

Seba thanked him for the gift very politely, and his mother received Max warmly, telling him he could stay and sleep on the sofa. But he didn't want to stay. He sipped a little of the bitter mate she offered him, devoured a cheese empanada, and headed back to the station to catch the 12:30 bus. "I'm really busy, I have a ton of work," he said before getting into the same taxi that had brought him there. He curtly ruffled Sebastián's hair and gave him a kiss on the forehead.

Once he was alone, Sebastián set up the computer and confirmed what he already suspected: it was notably inferior, any way you looked at it, to the one he already had. He laughed about it a lot with his stepdad after lunch. Then the two of them went down to the basement to find a place to store the computer, and that's where it's been ever since, waiting, perhaps, for better days ahead.

Part 3

National Institute

for Marcelo Montecinos

1

The teachers called us by our numbers on the list. I say that by way of apology: I don't even know my character's name. I remember 34 very well, though. I was always 45 back then. Because of the first letter of my last name, I enjoyed a more stable identity than the other kids. I still feel a certain familiarity with that number. It was good to be 45. Much better than being 15, for instance, or 27.

The first thing I remember about 34 is that he sometimes ate carrots during recess. His mother peeled them and arranged them harmoniously in a little Tupperware that he opened by cautiously loosening the corners. He applied the exact amount of force necessary, as if practicing a very difficult art. But more important than his taste for carrots was the fact that he had been held back: he was the only student in our grade who was repeating it.

For us, repeating a grade was shameful. We had never gotten close to that kind of failure in our short lives. We were eleven or twelve years old, we came from all kinds of backgrounds, and we had been selected to enter Chile's gargantuan and illustrious National Institute: our files were impeccable. But there was number 34: his existence was proof that failure was possible, and perhaps it wasn't even all that bad, because he wore his stigma with ease, as if he were, when it came down to it, perfectly happy to go back over the same subjects again. "You're a familiar face," a teacher would sometimes say sarcastically, and 34 would respond graciously: "Yes, sir, I'm repeating this grade. I'm the only one repeating in the class. But I'm sure that this year is going to go better for me."

Those first months at the National Institute were hell. The teachers made sure to tell us over and over how difficult the school was; they tried to make us regret coming there, tried to send us right back to our "little corner schoolhouses," as they said contemptuously, in that gargling tone of voice that terrified us instead of making us laugh.

I don't know if it's necessary to clarify that those teachers were some real sons of bitches. They did have names, first ones and last ones: the math teacher, Mr. Bernardo Aguayo, for example—he was a total son of a bitch. And the shop teacher, Mr. Eduardo Venegas. A real motherfucker. Neither time nor distance has dampened my rage. They were cruel and mediocre. Frustrated and stupid people. Obsequious Pinochetistas. Fucking assholes.

But I was talking about 34, and not those motherfucking bastards we had for teachers.

Number 34's behavior was not what you would expect from someone who was repeating a grade. You'd think that a kid who gets held back would be sullen, out of step with their new class, reluctant to join in, but 34 was always willing to experience things right along with us. He didn't suffer from that attachment to the past that makes kids who repeat grades into unhappy and melancholic characters, perpetually trailing along behind their classmates from the previous year, or waging a continuous battle against those who are supposedly to blame for their situation.

That was the strangest thing about 34: he wasn't resentful. Sometimes we would see him talking with teachers who were unknown to us, teachers from other seventh-grade classrooms. They were happy conversations, with lively gesticulations and pats on the back. He maintained cordial relations with the teachers who had failed him, it seemed.

We quaked every time 34 showed signs of his undeniable intelligence during class. But he never showed off; quite the contrary, he only chimed in to suggest new points of view, or to give his opinion on complex subjects. The things he said weren't written in the books, and we admired him for that, but admiring him felt like digging our own graves: if someone so smart had failed, it made it all the more likely that we would fail, too. We speculated behind his back about the real reasons he'd had to repeat: intricate family conflicts, long and painful illnesses. But deep down we knew that 34's problem was strictly academic—we knew that his failure would, tomorrow, be our own.

Once, he approached me out of the blue, looking both alarmed and happy. It took him some time to start talking, as if he had thought long and hard about what he was going to say to me. "You don't have anything to worry about," he finally blurted out. "I've been watching you, and I'm sure you're going to pass." It was so comforting to hear that. It really made me happy. It made me irrationally happy. 34 was, as they say, the voice of experience, and his evaluation brought relief.

Soon I found out that the same scene had been repeated with others in our class, and a rumor spread that 34 was messing with us. But then it occurred to us that this might be his way of instilling confidence. And we needed that confidence. The teachers tortured us daily, and report cards were disastrous for us all. There were almost no exceptions. We were all headed straight for the slaughterhouse.

The key was to figure out if 34 was giving us all the same message, or only a chosen few. It turned out there were seven students who still had not been absolved by 34, and they went into a state of panic. 38—or maybe 37, I'm not sure of his number—was one of the most worried. He couldn't stand the uncertainty. His desperation grew so intense that one day, defying the logic of the system, he went up to 34 and asked directly if he would pass. 34 seemed uncomfortable with the question. "Let me study you," he proposed. "I haven't been able to watch everyone—there are a lot of you. I'm sorry, but I haven't been paying you much attention."

You have to understand, 34 was not putting on airs. Absolutely not. There was a permanent whiff of honesty in his manner of speaking, and it was hard to question what he said. His frank gaze helped, too: he made sure to look you in the eyes, and he spaced out his words with brief but suspenseful pauses. A slow and mature rhythm beat within his words. "I haven't been able to watch everyone—there are a lot of you," he had told 38, and no one doubted this. Number 34 spoke oddly and he spoke seriously. Although perhaps back then we believed that in order to speak seriously, you had to speak oddly.

The next day 38 asked for his verdict, but 34 only answered with excuses, as if he wanted to hide—we thought—a painful truth. "Give me more time," he said. "I'm still not sure." By then we'd all given 38 up for lost, but a week later, after completing the observation period, 34 went up to him and said, to everyone's surprise: "Yes, you will pass. It's definite."

We were happy, of course, and we also celebrated on the following day, when he rescued the remaining six. But there was still something important to resolve: now all of the students had been blessed by 34, and it was unusual for everyone to pass. We did some investigating and found that never, in the almost two hundred years of the school's history, had all forty-five students in a seventh-grade class passed.

During the following, decisive months, 34 could tell we were starting to doubt his predictions, but he didn't acknowledge it: he went on faithfully eating his carrots, and he regularly spoke up in classes, volunteering his brave and engaging opinions. He knew we were watching him, that he was in the hot seat, but he treated us with the same warmth as always.

At the end of the year, when final exams came, we learned that 34 had hit the bull's-eye with his predictions. Four classmates had jumped ship early (including 38), and of the forty-one who remained, forty of us passed. The only one who didn't pass was, once again, 34.

On the last day of classes we went over to console him. He was sad, of course, but he didn't seem beside himself. "I was expecting it," he said. "I'm really bad at studying. Maybe

things will be better at a different school. They say that sometimes you have to just step aside. I think this is the moment
to step aside."

It hurt all of us to lose 34. That abrupt ending seemed, to us,
like an injustice. But then we saw him again the next year, falling in line with the seventh graders on the first day of class.
The school didn't allow students to repeat a grade twice, but
for 34 they had, for some reason, made an exception. There
were a few students who claimed it was unfair that 34 had gotten help from friends in high places. But most of us thought it
was good that he stayed—even though we were surprised that
he would want to go through that experience for a third time.

I went over to talk to him that same day. I tried to be
friendly, and he was cordial, too. He looked thinner, and you
could really see the age difference between him and his new
classmates. "I'm not 34 anymore," he told me finally, in that
solemn tone that by then I knew well. "I'm grateful to you for
checking on me, but 34 doesn't exist anymore," he said. "Now
I'm 29, and I have to get used to my new reality. I'd rather be
part of my new class and make new friends. It's not healthy
to get stuck in the past."

I guess he was right. Every once in a while we'd see him
from afar, hanging out with his new classmates or talking
with those same teachers who had failed him the year before.
I think that year he finally managed to pass, but I don't know
if he stayed at the school much longer. Little by little, we lost
track of him.

2

One afternoon, when they came back from gym class, they found the following message written on the board:

Augusto Pinochet is:

A) a motherfucker
B) a son of a bitch
C) an asshole
D) a piece of shit
E) all of the above

And underneath it said:

IOP

It had to be erased, but there was no time, because right then Villagra, the natural sciences teacher, entered the room. There was a nervous murmur and some timid laughter, and then the absolute silence that always reigned in Villagra's classes. Villagra looked at the board for a few long minutes, his back to the students. The writing, with its firm strokes and perfect calligraphy, was not that of a twelve-year-old boy. Moreover, it wasn't exactly common for seventh graders to be members of the IOP, the Institutional Oppositional Party.

With the same gravity, the same theatricality as always, Villagra went to the door and looked out to make sure he wasn't being spied on. Then he picked up the eraser and slowly started to erase the options one by one, but before he got to the last answer, "all of the above," he stopped to brush away the chalk dust that had fallen onto his jacket, and he let out a cough that resounded exaggeratedly. Then, from the last row, Bonner—better known to his classmates, of course, as Boner—asked if the correct answer was (e). Villagra looked at the ceiling as if searching for inspiration, and his face really did take on an expression of enlightenment. "Yes, but the question is poorly designed," he said. He explained that options (a) and (b) were practically identical, as were (c) and (d), so it was obvious, by default, that the answer was (e).

"So the right answer is 'all of the above'?" asked González Reyes.

"As I said, it is the correct answer by default. Open your books to page eighty, please."

"Aaaaahhhhhh," said the boys.

"But sir, what do you think of Pinochet?" insisted a different González, González Torres (there were six boys named González in the class).

"That doesn't matter," he said, serene and decisive. "I'm the natural sciences teacher. I don't talk about politics."

3

I remember the cramp in my right hand after history class, because Godoy dictated for the entire two hours. He taught us Athenian democracy by dictating as one does in a dictatorship.

I remember Lavoisier's Law, but I remember the law of the jungle much better.

———

I remember Aguayo saying that "in Chile, people are lazy, they just don't want to work; Chile is full of opportunities."

I remember Aguayo failing us, but offering make-up classes with his daughter, who was beautiful, but we didn't like her, because in her face we could see the dog-like face of her father.

I remember Veragua wearing white socks to school and Aguayo telling him: "You are trash."

I remember Veragua's long hair, and his big green eyes that filled with tears as he stared at the ground, in silence, humiliated. He never came back to school again.

I remember Venegas, the head teacher, telling us the following Monday: "Veragua's parents withdrew him. He couldn't hack it."

I remember Elizabeth Azócar teaching us to write during the final hours of each Friday. I was in love with Elizabeth Azócar.

I remember Martínez Gallegos, and Hugo Puebla, and Álvaro Tabilo.

———

I remember Gonzalo Mario Cordero Lafferte, who used to tell jokes during study hall. If any teachers happened to walk by, he would pretend we were studying French: *la pipe*, *la table*, *la voiture*.

I remember that we never complained. How stupid, to complain—we had to bear it all like men. But the idea of manliness was confused: sometimes it meant bravery, other times indolence.

I remember when someone stole the money I was going to use to make the optional annual PTA payment.

Later I found out who stole it, and he knew I knew. Every time we looked at each other, we said, with our eyes: I know you robbed me, I know you know I robbed you.

I remember the list of Chilean presidents who had studied at my school. I remember that when teachers reeled off that list, they omitted the name of Salvador Allende.

I remember saying "my school" with pride.

———

I remember the Subordinate Noun Clause and the Subordinate Adjective/Relative Clause.

I remember the vocabulary exercises, which were full of strange words that we'd repeat later, dying of laughter: commiseration, skirmish, bauble, knickknack, iridescent, vindicate, craggy, succinct.

I remember that Soto got dropped off at school by the chauffeur who drove for his father, a military man.

I remember that the English teacher gave a bad grade to a student who had lived in Chicago for ten years, and later she said, ashamed, "I didn't know he was a gringo."

I remember stupid teachers and brilliant teachers.

I remember the most brilliant of all, Ricardo Ferrada, who, during the first class of the year, wrote a Henry Miller quote on the board that changed my life.

I remember teachers who wanted to sink us and teachers who wanted to save us. Teachers who thought they were Mr. Keating. Teachers who thought they were God. Teachers who thought they were Nietzsche.

———

I remember the group of homosexuals senior year. There were five or six, they always sat together, and talked only to one another. The biggest of them wrote me beautiful love letters.

They never played any sports, and the few times they went out during breaks, they got teased and hit. So they stayed in the classroom instead, talking or fighting among themselves. They shouted "Bitch!" and threw their backpacks at one another's faces or to the floor.

I remember one morning during study hall, we were warming up for a math test with no teachers in the room, and the letter writer was talking nonstop with his seatmate. Carlos shouted at him: "Shut up, you fat faggot!"

I remember how he stood up, enraged, exaggerating his effeminate gestures, and retorted: "Don't you ever call me fat again."

I remember smoking marijuana during recess, in the basement, with Andrés Chamorro, Cristián Villablanca, and Camilo Dattoli.

———

I remember Pato Parra, one of four people who repeated junior year. I remember his drawings.

I remember he sat at the first desk in the middle row, and the only thing he did during class was draw.

He never looked at the teachers—he was always hunched over, concentrated on his drawing from behind Coke-bottle glasses, his hair falling over the paper.

I remember the quick head movement that Pato Parra made to keep his hair from messing up the drawing.

None of the teachers scolded him, not for his long hair, nor for his absolute indifference to their classes. And if one of them ever asked why he wasn't participating, he would apologize dryly and politely, leaving no room for discussion.

I only got to know him a little, we only talked a few times. I remember one morning that I spent sitting next to him, looking at his drawings, which were perfect, almost always realistic: comics about unemployment, about poverty, all depicted straightforwardly, honestly.

———

I remember he drew a picture of me that morning. I still have the drawing, but I don't know where it is.

I'm not sure if it was in June or July, but I remember it was a winter morning when we found out that Pato Parra had committed suicide.

I remember the cold in the Puente Alto cemetery. I remember the teachers trying to explain what had happened. And I remember wishing that they would shut up, shut up, shut up. And the emptiness afterward, all year, when we looked at the first desk in the middle row.

I remember the teacher's assistant telling us that life went on.

I remember that life went on, but not in the same way.

I remember we all cried in the school bus, which we called the Caleuche, on the way back.

I remember walking with Hugo Puebla across the playground soccer field, our arms around each other, crying.

———

I remember the phrase that Pato Parra wrote, on his bedroom wall, before killing himself: "My final cry to the world: Shit."

4

I remember the final months at that school, in 1993: the desire for it all to be over soon. I was nervous—we all were—waiting for the big test, which we had spent six years preparing for. Because that's what the National Institute was: a college prep that lasted six years.

One morning, we exploded. We got into a fight, all of us shouting and hitting: an eruption of absolute violence whose origins we did not understand. It happened a lot, but this time we felt a kind of rage or impotence or sadness that had never emerged before. As a result of our outburst, Washington Musa, the Inspector General of Sector One, paid our class a visit. I remember that name, Washington Musa. Whatever became of him? How little I care.

Musa adopted the same tone as always, the tone we heard from so many teachers and inspectors during those years. He told us that we were privileged, that we had received an excellent education. That we'd been taught by the best teachers in Chile. And all for free, he emphasized. "But you people aren't going to get anywhere, I don't know how you've survived this school. You humanities people have destroyed the National Institute," he said. None of it hurt us, since we had heard that reprimand, that monologue, many times before. We looked at the floor or at our notebooks. We were closer to laughter than tears, laughter that would have been bitter or sarcastic or pretentious, but laughter still.

And nonetheless, no one laughed. While Musa droned on, the silence was absolute. Suddenly he started to cruelly berate Javier García Guarda. Javier was perhaps the most silent and timid boy in the class. He didn't get bad grades, or good ones, either, and his file was clean: not a single negative mark, not a single positive note. But Musa, furious, was humiliating him, and we didn't know why. Little by little we understood that Javier had dropped his pen. That was all. And Musa thought he'd done it on purpose, or he didn't think about it, but he took advantage of the incident to focus all his rage onto García Guarda: "I don't even want to know what kind of education you got from your parents," he was saying. "You don't deserve to be at this school."

I stood up and defended my classmate, or rather, I stood up and offended Musa. I told him, "Shut up, sir, shut up right now, you have no idea what you're talking about. You're humiliating him and it's not fair, sir."

An even more intense silence fell.

Musa was tall, solidly built, and bald. In addition to his work at the Institute, he ran a jewelry shop, and he greatly enhanced his income through sales at the school: every so often he would stop in the hallway to praise brooches, watches, or necklaces that he himself had sold to the teachers. With the students he was mean, icy, despotic, as dictated by the nature of his position: his reprimands and punishments were legendary. His defining characteristic, I thought then and still think now, was arrogance. But when I challenged him, Musa didn't know what to do, how to react.

"My office, both of you," he said, thoroughly annoyed.

I remember that on the way to Musa's office, Mejías came over to encourage us. I had acted bravely, but maybe it wasn't bravery, or it was the indolent side of bravery: I was simply fed up, I didn't care. Despite how close we were to finishing at the Institute, I would have been happy to go back that very day to "the corner schoolhouse." I thought I had found an excuse to get myself expelled. But I also knew they weren't going to expel me. There were teachers who cared about me, who would protect me. Musa knew that.

"As for you, García, I'm going to think very seriously about whether to let you walk at graduation," said Musa. "Tomorrow, first thing, I'm going to have a talk with your parents." Only then, when I looked at García Guarda's black and weepy eyes, did I realize I had made everything worse, that the thing should have ended with a reprimand, with one more humiliating moment. I realized that García Guarda would have preferred that, but because of my intervention, it had all escalated. They only involved parents in the worst of cases, because at my school, parents didn't exist. "Expel me instead," I said, but I knew that wasn't how this went: his way of punishing me was to torture García. I almost insisted again, but I held back, knowing I would only fan the flames.

"I'm not going to expel you, nor will I keep you from attending the ceremony," Musa told me, and again I thought about how unfair it was for me to receive a lesser punishment than García. And I also thought that I couldn't care less about a stupid graduation ceremony. But maybe I did care. I felt indestructible. Rage made me indestructible. But not only rage. There was also a blind confidence or a kind of stubbornness that had always been with me. Because I spoke softly, but I was strong. Because I speak softly, but I'm strong. Because I never shout, but I'm strong.

"I shouldn't let you go to that ceremony, I should expel you right now," he told me. "But I'm not going to." Thirty seconds went by, but Musa hadn't finished. I was still looking out of the corner of my eye at the tears sliding down García Guarda's face. I remember that he wrote poems, too, but he didn't show them to people like I did—he didn't play at the spectacle of poetry. We weren't exactly friends, but we talked every once in a while, we respected each other.

"I'm not going to keep you from graduating, I'm not going to expel you, but I'm going to tell you something that you will never, in your whole life, forget," Musa said. He emphasized the word "never," and then the words "whole life," and he repeated this phrase another two times.

"I'm not going to keep you from graduating, I'm not going to expel you, but I'm going to tell you something that you will never in your whole life forget." I don't remember what he told me. I forgot it immediately. I sincerely don't know what Musa told me then. I remember that I looked him in the face, bravely or indolently, but I didn't retain a single one of his words.

I Smoked
Very Well

for Álvaro Enrigue
and
Valeria Luiselli

The treatment lasts for ninety days. Today is the fourteenth day. According to the information pamphlet, I get one last cigarette.
The last cigarette of my life.
I just smoked it.

It lasted six minutes and seven seconds. The last smoke ring dissolved before it reached the ceiling. I drew something in the ash (my heart?).

I don't know if I'm opening or closing parentheses.

What I feel is something like pain and defeat. But I look for positive signs. This is right, it's what I have to do.

I was good at smoking; I was one of the best. I smoked very well.

I smoked naturally, fluidly, happily. With a great deal of elegance. With passion.

And it's been easy, unexpectedly. The first days, almost without realizing it, I went from sixty to forty cigarettes. And then from forty to twenty. When I realized that my quota was going down so fast, I smoked several in a row, as if trying to get back in shape or reclaim my ranking. But I didn't enjoy those cigarettes.

This morning I only smoked two, and I didn't even want them, really—I was just taking advantage of what I was allowed. Neither of those cigarettes felt complete, or true.

+ + + + +

Nineteen days, five without smoking.

Up to now there's been nothing dramatic in the process, but I'm searching for a hidden compartment, something else to train my eyes on.

The speed of the whole thing is alarming. As is the docility of my organism. Champix invaded my body, and there was nothing to oppose it. In spite of my debilitating headaches, I used to think of myself as a strong man—but this drug was able to change something essential in me.

It's absurd to think that the medicine is going to do nothing but turn me away from this one habit. Surely it will also distance me from other things that I haven't yet discovered. And it will carry them so far away from me I won't be able to see them.

I'm going to change a lot, and that is something I don't like. I want to change, but in a different way. I don't know what I'm saying.

I feel perplexed, and bruised. It's as though someone were gradually erasing my memory of all the information related to cigarettes. And that strikes me as sad.

I am a very old computer. I'm an old but not entirely broken computer. Someone touches my face and keyboard with a kitchen rag. And it hurts.

✦   ✦   ✦   ✦   ✦

For over twenty years, the first thing I did when I got up was smoke two cigarettes in a row. I think that, strictly speaking, that's why I woke up, that's what I woke up for. I was happy to find, in the first lucid blinking of my eyes, that I could smoke immediately. And only after the first drag did I really wake up.

Last fall I tried to fight the urge, to put off the day's first cigarette as long as I could. It was disastrous. I stayed in bed until 11:30, disheartened, and at 11:31, I finally inhaled.

It's day number twenty-one of the treatment—and the seventh without smoking. The clouds scribble on the sky.

Cigarettes are the punctuation marks of life.

✦ ✦ ✦ ✦ ✦

I spend the afternoon reading *Migraine*, by Oliver Sacks. From the beginning, he warns that there is no infallible cure for migraines. In most cases, patients are pilgrims who roam from doctor to doctor, from drug to drug. That's what I am, and what I have been for too many years now.

The book demonstrates that migraines are interesting and not devoid of beauty (the beauty that throbs within the inexplicable). But what good is it to know that you suffer from a beautiful or interesting illness?

Sacks dedicates only a few pages to the kind of headache that I suffer from (*my* headache): it is the most savage kind of them all, but not the most common. Mine has many different names: migrainous neuralgia, histamine headache, Horton's cephalalgia, Harris-Horton's disease, cluster headaches. But much more revealing is its nickname: suicide headache. When you're in its clutches, that's the urge that takes over. More than a few patients have tried to alleviate the pain by banging their heads against the wall. I know I have.

It hurts on one side of the head, specifically in the area that falls under the influence of the trigeminal nerve. It's a feeling of trepidation accompanied by photophobia, phonophobia, watery eyes, facial sweat, and nasal congestion, among other symptoms. I memorize the numbers, recite the statistics: only ten out of every hundred thousand people suffer from cluster headaches. And eight or nine of those ten people are men.

The cycles, the clusters, are unleashed without any apparent trigger, and they last for two to four months. The pain explodes uncontrollably, especially at night. All you can do is surrender. You also have to accept with a brave face the variety of advice your friends will give you, all of it useless. Until one fine day, they disappear—the headaches, not the friends, although some friends will also get sick of your headaches, because during those months you'll never be around, inevitably focused only on yourself.

The joy of being back to normal can last for one or two years. And just when you think you're finally cured for good—when you think of the headaches the way you'd think of a former enemy you've come to appreciate a little, even care for—the pain comes back: at first shyly, then with its usual insolence.

I remember an episode where Gregory House treats a patient complaining of cluster headaches straightaway with hallucinogenic mushrooms. "Nothing else works," says House, scandalizing his medical team, as usual. But even mushrooms don't work on me. Nor does sleeping without a pillow, or yoga, or greedily welcoming the acupuncturist's needles. Not reexamining my entire life to the beat of psychoanalysis (and discovering many things, some of them atrocious, but nothing that would banish the pain). Not giving up cheese, or wine, or almonds, or pistachios. Not swallowing a pharmacy-and-a-half of aggressive medicines. None of that has freed me from the sudden, insidious blooming of pain. The only thing I hadn't tried was this: quitting smoking. And of course, to make things worse, Sacks says there is no proof of the relationship between migraines and cigarettes. As I underlined that passage, I felt dizzy, desperate.

The thing that worries me most is that right now, I'm in the midst of a truce with my illness. I could quit smoking, think that everything is fine, and then have a cluster within the year. My neurologist, however, is positive that quitting will cure me.

He studied general medicine for seven years, and then studied his specialty for another three. All of that so he could tell me: Smoking is bad for your health.

+ + + + +

Day twenty-six of the treatment, day twenty-six minus fourteen without smoking.

Other than a slight nausea that quickly disappears, I haven't experienced any major issues. I've just looked over the list of side effects again, and I've got none of them. Just two "headaches"—I'm against ironic quotation marks, but they feel justified here. Such ridiculous little headaches—the kind you can take aspirin for. I have no respect for them.

According to the Champix information brochure, in addition to the nausea and cephalalgia, possible side effects include abnormal dreams, insomnia, drowsiness, dizziness, vomiting, flatulence, dysgeusia, diarrhea, constipation, and stomach pain. The abnormal dreams don't bother me, because my dreams have never been normal. But I'm troubled by the bit about insomnia and drowsiness; I wonder if they can happen at the same time, like love and hate. Dysgeusia (change in taste) is great. I would love to excuse myself some time by saying, "I'm sorry, but I have dysgeusia." What supreme elegance.

There are also those rumors about Champix that tend to

appear in the newspaper's science section, which I don't give any credit to because I don't believe in the paper's science section. What a tremendous tall tale: on Monday they report on important studies at prestigious universities about the benefits of wine or almonds, and on Wednesday they say that both are bad for you. I remember that verse from Nicanor Parra: "Bread is bad for you / all foods are bad for you." It's like the horoscope section: last week it said the same thing on Monday for Libra that it said on Saturday for Pisces.

In any case, the rumors are that many people who take Champix start having suicidal thoughts. I read online that in the span of a year, 227 cases of attempted suicide were reported, along with 397 cases of psychotic disorders, 525 cases of violent behavior, 41 cases of homicidal thoughts, 60 cases of paranoia, and 55 cases of hallucinations. I don't believe any of that.

My big problem up to now has been my hands. I don't know what to do with my hands. I hold on to my pockets, railings, my cheeks, cellophane wrapping, cups. Most of all to cups: I get drunk faster now, which isn't really a problem—everyone around me understands.

It bothers me, that unanimous approval of what some people call—cigarette in hand—"my brave decision."

"I admire you," one horrible person told me today, and then added, with a studied, somber expression: "I sure couldn't do it."

+ + + + +

"Are you smoking?"

"No, Mom, I'm praying."

It's day thirty-five of the treatment, day twenty-one without smoking.

I had lunch with Jovana downtown. She can't believe that I've stopped smoking. She smokes happily and I am envious, although I must admit that, secretly, I have a newfound feeling of satisfaction, even if it's ambiguous, because this hasn't required any effort on my part: the medicine, quite simply, took over.

"We are the only minority that no one defends," Jovana told me, laughing, speaking with that warm, thick voice of hers, that smoker's voice. Right away she added, as if on behalf of all the world's smokers: "We were counting on you."

Then she told me it was impossible to remember her father, who died recently, without a cigarette between his lips. He would sometimes go out very early, unexpectedly, and when someone asked where he was going, he would answer, energized: "To kill the morning!" What great wisdom, I think. To walk: to just walk and smoke to kill the morning.

I think that I am reeducating myself in some unknown aspect of life.

I move some old files around and find this note from a year ago: "I have a cut on my finger that keeps me from smoking well. Everything else is okay."

+ + + + +

What for a smoker is nonfiction, for a non-smoker is fiction. That majestic story by Julio Ramón Ribeyro, for example, about the smoker who desperately jumps out the window to rescue a pack of cigarettes. Years later, very ill, his wife keeping a vigilant watch over him, he escapes to the beach every day to unearth, with the skill of an anxious puppy, the pack of cigarettes he had hidden in the sand. Non-smokers don't understand these stories. They think that they're exaggerated, they give them short shrift. A smoker, on the other hand, treasures them.

"What would have become of me if the cigarette hadn't been invented?" writes Ribeyro in 1958, in a letter to his brother. "It's three in the afternoon and I've already smoked thirty." Then he explains, quoting Gide, that writing is "an act that complements smoking." And in a later message, he signs off by saying: "I only have one cigarette left, and so I declare this letter over."

I could smoke without writing, of course, but I couldn't write without smoking. That's why I'm scared now: What if I quit writing? The only thing that I've been able to write since I quit are these notes.

+ + + + +

I've just arrived in Punta Arenas. For the first time ever, I was able to read on the plane. Because I started traveling when I was already grown up, I was never on a flight where you could smoke, and if I couldn't smoke, I couldn't read, either. The presence of ashtrays in the armrests made me nervous.

I remembered that brilliant and unequivocal phrase of Italo Svevo's: "Reading a novel without smoking is impossible."

But it's possible, it is. I don't remember anything I read, though. I read badly. I don't know if I've just read a good novel badly or a bad novel well. But I did read, it's possible.

I just closed this document without mentioning my relapse. Marvelous, you lied to your journal, asshole. I have to record it. It was in the Punta Arenas cemetery. I wanted to go there to remember a poem of Lihn's that talks about "a peace struggling to shatter itself." It's the impression that remains after looking at the cypresses there ("this double row of bowing cypresses"), the inspired mausoleums, the cradle-shaped graves of dead babies, the headstones with words in other languages, the meticulously tended alcoves, the miraculously fresh flowers. I looked at the sea while Galo Ghigliotto played with some blocks of ice in the birdbath, and my host, Óscar Barrientos, visited some family graves. Then we left, walking in silence. I was thinking about the peace Lihn wrote about, that peace that struggles to shatter. And suddenly, offhandedly, I asked Galo for a cigarette, and only on the fourth or fifth drag did I remember that I had quit smoking. Only then did I taste the bitterness, feel the intense aversion. I finished it, but it took effort.

———

I really don't smoke anymore, I think.
I really don't think anymore, I smoke.

The medicine won't let me smoke.

+ + + +

Day forty/twenty-six.

I have Sacks's book in my bag, underlined, ready to show the doctor that there's no proof of a relationship between smoking and cluster headaches. "Sacks is entertaining," the neurologist replies. But says he's not sure he's read him. I point out the contradiction in what he has just said: how does he know that Sacks is entertaining if he hasn't read him? He doesn't listen. I get aggressive. "Doctors used to read," I tell him. "In the past, doctors were cultured."

He doesn't seem offended, but he looks at me the way someone would look at an alien. Someone like the doctor, not someone like me. I would never look at an alien like that, so obviously surprised.

I offer to lend him Sacks's book, but he declines. Now he does get mad. He lectures me like I'm a child. He rails against cigarettes with such insistence that I feel like he is talking shit about someone I love, someone who doesn't deserve this kind of slander. But what I want most in the world is for my head to never hurt again. I'll go on with the treatment, of course I will. I have faith.

I remember those verses that Sergio liked, from a poem by

Ernst Jandl, I think: "The doctor has told me / that I cannot kiss."

As for me, the doctor has told me I cannot smoke.

+ + + + +

At eleven years old, more or less, I became, almost simultaneously, a voracious reader and a promising smoker. Then, in my first years at university, a more lasting bond formed between reading and tobacco. In those days Kurt was reading Heinrich Böll, and since all I ever did back then was imitate Kurt in an attempt to be his friend, I got my hands on *The Clown*, a very beautiful and bitter novel in which the characters smoked all the time—on every page, or at least every page-and-a-half. And every time they lit their cigarettes, I would light mine, as if that were my way of taking part in the novel. Maybe that's what the literary theorists meant when they talked about the active reader: a reader who suffers when the characters suffer, who is happy when they are happy, who smokes when they smoke.

I went on reading Böll's novels, and every time someone smoked in them, I would smoke, too. And I think that in *Billiards at Half-Past Nine* and *And Never Said a Word* and *House without Guardians*, the books I read next, the characters also smoked a lot, although I don't really remember. In any case, by the time I finished those novels I had become a compulsive smoker. Or, to put it more precisely, a professional smoker.

I'm not stupid enough to claim that it was all Heinrich

Böll's fault. No: it was thanks to him. How frivolous all this must sound. Thanks to those novels, I understood my country and my own history better. Those novels changed my life. But will I be able to read them again without smoking?

In a venerable passage from his *Irish Journal*, Böll himself says it was impossible for him to watch a movie in the cinema if he couldn't smoke. My dear dead friend, you have no idea how many times, because of my desire to smoke, I have fled the theater in the middle of the movie.

✦ ✦ ✦ ✦ ✦

Fiftieth/thirty-sixth.

It took two cigarettes to get from my house to the pool hall. In 1990, when I was fourteen years old. Two cigarettes: the first when I left the house, followed by a pause, and then the second, which I would finish just before entering the pool hall on Primera Transversal, where I'd light another one that was not the third, but rather the first of a long night of chalk and trick shots. At any given moment there was a lit cigarette hanging from someone's lips. (We had a saying that went "Chalk and keep calm." I could use a little chalk and calm now.)

Tennis, too. It took me two and a half cigarettes to get to my cousin Rodrigo's house, and then one more for us to reach an empty lot where some generous or forgetful person had set up a net. Every once in a while we stopped the game to smoke, and I remember that on several occasions we smoked while we played. He always beat me at tennis, but I always won at the extreme sport of smoking.

✦ ✦ ✦ ✦ ✦

Another relapse, last night, in Buenos Aires, all because of this new affability I've contracted.

My newfound affability makes me get too close too soon, like those people who go in for a hug when you least expect it. I'm imitating people I've always looked down on. That's what I'm turning into: I now quash my anxiety by expressing premature emotions. But I don't pounce on just anyone—I approach huggable people, people who, according to my first impressions, seem to deserve that closeness. My gesture is not exactly a hug, either, but more like a halting movement accompanied by undignified nervous laughter.

I was with Maize, Matron, Libreville, Merlin, Canella, Valeria, and several other recent acquaintances whom, before long, I was already thinking of as close friends. On top of the beer—which I can drink again, after unfairly blaming it for the headaches for years—there was an important factor contributing to my euphoria: the happiness of the tourist, the joy of passing through. From the comfortable sideline, I followed the terrible discussions about the local literary goings-on. They confronted each other, really going for it, invoking diffuse but legitimate principles, and miraculously, a sort of harmony or camaraderie prevailed. I demonstrated my gratitude through obedience: I wrote down the titles of all the books they recommended on a napkin—which, in a regrettable moment of carelessness, I used to wipe my mouth—I ate some atrociously greasy food, and I took each sip of beer with an urgency that matched theirs.

Suddenly an interest in my process arose, and I found myself explaining, in my awkward Chilean dialect, that I had stopped smoking, not by choice but by medical prescription, because of my malady. Oddly, no one at the table started talking about how they suffered or had suffered from headaches, which is the natural course that conversation takes. I noticed that they were focusing a lot on my way of speaking, but then the critic from Rosario or Córdoba—a sullen but somehow endearing guy who until then had participated intermittently in the conversation (sometimes he seemed interested, but most of the time he observed us with a sneer of disdain)—looked at me with his crazy, shining eyes and said, "Do me the favor of smoking again, Chileno." Maize supported him, Matron seconded it, Libreville too, and soon they were all shouting: "Come on, Chileno, have another smoke. Do it for Chile."

I obeyed. In a split second I had grabbed, lit, and taken a drag of a Marlboro Red. It was horrible, but the second one tasted a little better. My concession brought us back to normal, and the Rosarian critic—who could have been from Córdoba or Salta—started in on a story about his experiences with group sex. At a certain point I thought his true goal was to take us all to bed, but really he just wanted to talk about the details of his sex life for a while. Very soon, as if sticking to a capricious script, he resumed his default state of intermittent interlocutor.

Last night's final cigarette was accompanied by a couple of whiskeys that Pedrito Maize treated me to in the hotel bar. I woke up at noon, with barely enough time to pack my suitcase and head to the airport. The dreaded day-after has been doubly bad in this case; it's as though I can distinguish the layers, the different levels of hangover. The fallout from the alcohol is slight, but the aftereffect of the eight or nine cigarettes has stuck around. Maybe the medicine prolongs that sense of disgust, as a kind of punishment. From now on, I'll find a way to keep my new affability in check.

+ + + + +

Walking down Agustinas this morning, I saw a man approximately my age and height and also my coloring, who was smoking as he walked. I watched him take a drag of his cigarette, and for an instant the movement struck me as very odd. It was a long drag, as though in slow motion. Suddenly, I wanted to absorb or devour his face. I felt astonishment, then revulsion. The man was disgusting to me. Later on—soon, right away, but later—I understood that he revolted me because we were so similar.

We resembled each other completely, with the exception of four obvious differences: the color of his pants (I would never wear that "waffle cone" shade), the hook-shaped earring that hung from his left ear, his clean-shaven face (versus my growing stubble), and, of course, that cigarette in his mouth, which I always used to have, too.

+ + + +

I read on the cover of a book of Fogwill's:

"I sailed a lot, I planted many trees, and I had four children. As I finish editing the works that will make up this volume, I await the birth of the fifth. To think in the sun, to sail, and to produce and serve children are the activities that feel best to me: I'm confident I will go on repeating them."

Then I remember that text of Nicanor Parra's, "Mission Accomplished":

> Trees planted 17
> Children 6
> Works published 7
> Total 30

I won't commit the folly of going over my own life in those terms. But yesterday, at the office, Jovana and I were playing around with Excel, and we got caught up in some dangerous accounting. Now I have the approximate calculation of how many cigarettes I smoked in my life. And the total amount of money I spent on cigarettes. I'm keeping this notebook as a kind of therapy, but I don't dare write those numbers down here. I'm ashamed. I do a little division and determine that the monthly amount I've spent on cigarettes, for years now, is roughly equivalent to a mortgage. I am a person who has chosen to smoke rather than have a house. I'm someone who has smoked a house.

✦ ✦ ✦ ✦

Another relapse. The details aren't important. I was desperate, and smoking didn't solve the problem (because the problem doesn't have a solution). I felt disgusted again, but at least I managed to distract myself.

+ + + + +

Another relapse: a prolongation of the one before, really. A semi-headache that I couldn't soothe with the old medications. I don't think it's a cluster, the pain is different. Also, my throat hurts, and my stomach, and my whole body.

"Sir, the tobacco on the tip of your cigarette is on fire," said a character of Macedonio's.

+ + + + +

Day I don't know which of the year two thousand and never.

I remember when I was living in a godforsaken room in Madrid, in Vallecas, on Calle de la Marañosa, sharing an apartment with three Spanish security guards (two men and a very pregnant woman who worked at the Barajas airport) and an Argentine ex-cop who was trying his luck. One morning, when I had a fever and had almost completely lost my voice, I lit a harsh Ducados cigarette, looked out the window, and recited aloud, in a tempered but exhilarated cry, Enrique Lihn's poem about Madrid.

> I don't know what the hell I'm doing here
> Old, tired, sick, and thoughtful.

The Spanish I was spawned with,
Father of so many literary vices
and from which I cannot free myself,
may have brought me to this city
to make me suffer what I deserve:
a soliloquy in a dead language.

It was as if I were greeting everyone and no one from my balcony, taking revenge on the city, but also, somehow, in my own way, courting it. I think that Ducados is on the list of the best cigarettes I've ever smoked.

+   +   +   +   +

"Darkness smoked with resolve," says a poem by R. Merino. The image is exact: the last ember, raising one's head to keep that bit of fire from falling, to avoid the disaster of losing it in the blankets and having to fumble around like a blind person, trying to put the cinder out. The danger of pulling a Clarice Lispector.

Another, compassionate line by Merino: "The one you smoke right now is all there is." Onetti in bed without cigarettes, furious, bad-humored, writing *The Well*. Existentialism, my ass—it was just a lack of tobacco. "I've smoked my cigarette to the end, unmoving."

I stopped smoking because of my clusters, but maybe that wasn't the main reason. The thing is, I'm cowardly and ambitious. I'm such a coward that I want to live longer. What an absurd thing, really: to want to live longer. As if I were, for example, happy.

I've finished the pills now—day ninety has come and gone. And I've stopped counting the days. I don't smoke anymore. Now I say it with certainty: No, I don't smoke. I want to smoke, but it's an ideological desire, not a physical one.

Because life without cigarettes is not any better. And the fucking headaches will come back sooner or later, whether or not I smoke.

✛ ✛ ✛ ✛ ✛

"Violent headache, but rather happy," notes Katherine Mansfield in her journal. Does she mean the headache is violent, but less so than usual, and thus pleasant? I don't get it.

Jazmín Lolas interviews Armando Uribe:
"You've never worried that cigarettes will kill you?"
"You know, I don't care; I don't support the idea that human beings, on average, should live so many years."

✛ ✛ ✛ ✛ ✛

The bestselling Mexican author Fernanda Familiar—TV star, blogger, and close friend of Gabriel García Márquez—

strolls around the Lima Book Fair with an electronic cigarette. It's the newest invention for quitting smoking, and right now it's the product I desire most. They don't sell them at the fair, unfortunately, and I hear they're expensive. What's more, I've already quit smoking. How idiotic: now I can't even try to quit smoking.

Not only did I quit smoking, I also quit trying to quit smoking.

For two hundred soles—approximately seven double pisco sours, extra large—I buy first editions of *Agua que no has de beber* by Antonio Cisneros and *Los elementos del desastre* by Álvaro Mutis, fortuitous finds that would justify any trip. But I don't read them. It seems that I no longer like books.

I should say, copying Pessoa: "I've reached Santiago, but not a conclusion."

Yesterday some people asked me what, in my opinion, was the main problem with Chilean literature. Now, first of all, it's pretty absurd that a hallway conversation can lead to a question like that. Hallway conversations are pretty much doomed to fail anyway, it seems to me, but I answered, with conviction, that the problem with Chilean literature was the custom of writing *cigarrillo* instead of *cigarro*. In Chile no one says *cigarrillo*, we say *cigarro*, I argued, as if pounding on an imaginary table, but Chilean authors always write *cigarrillo*, and I ended with this absolutely demagogic sentence: "I am a writer who writes *cigarro*."

The declaration had an immediate effect. They seemed to approve of it, but the conversation went downhill from there.

If there are more than four people in a conversation, it never ends well, especially if it's taking place in a hallway. I have to accept, of course, that I'm depressed and a little irritable. My own behavior exasperates me.

✛ ✛ ✛ ✛ ✛

Pulling an all-nighter, as they say. Nights without sleeping, spent reading or writing, the ashtray overflowing. Just before dawn, I'd be putting out cigarettes in the dregs of my coffee cup, each one the last, until the cup was full. A sort of horrific pincushion that I remember now with nostalgia.

How old was I when I read *Zeno's Conscience*? I think I was twenty or twenty-one. I have almost never laughed so much, although at the time, I thought you weren't supposed to laugh at books. "Seeing as it harms me, I'll never smoke again, but first, I'd like to do it one last time."

"Everything is infinitely lamer now," Andrés Braithwaite confessed to me two years ago, when he was on Champix. He looked defenseless, a timid puppy barking at the abyss. Then he told me that, without smoking, no book was good—he didn't enjoy reading anymore. I saw him again months later, and he was so handsome when he lit a cigarette and said, looking me in the eyes: "I'm cured." That afternoon my friend talked to me about fabulous authors he had just discovered, about unthinkable novels and brilliant poems. He had regained his passion, his roguishness, and his gentility. And the love for the vibration of his own voice. And his beauty.

Today, at some point, I felt this: an orphan relief. And I accepted that it's true, that everything is infinitely lamer. Literature, for sure. And life, above all.

I am a person who doesn't smoke, because of the invasive effect of a chemical that ruined his spirit and his life. I am a person who doesn't even know if he's going to go on writing, because he wrote in order to smoke and now he doesn't smoke; he read in order to smoke and now he doesn't smoke. I am a person who no longer makes anything up. Who just writes down what happens, as if it could interest anyone to know that I'm sleepy, that I'm drunk, and that I hate Rafa Araneda with all my soul.

Structural jam: in the pool halls, there's always a table where there's not enough space to get a good shot at the ball. That's called a structural jam.

That's what my life is like now.

Last night I wrote this beginning of a tango:

> Sad and serene
> expecting nothing
> maybe one day
> no sun and no rain

> I can look with ease
> upon the ashtray
> my voice now gutted
> of light and of love

I like the image of the ashtray, empty as never before, as now: incomprehensibly empty. What a terrible tango, anyway.

✦ ✦ ✦ ✦ ✦

Cigarettes are the punctuation marks of life. Now I live without punctuation, without rhythm. My life is a stupid avant-garde poem.

I live without cigarettes to mark a question. Without cigarettes that end as we dangerously or happily approach an answer. Or the absence of an answer.

Exclamation cigarettes. Ellipsis cigarettes. I would like to smoke with all the elegance of a semicolon.

To live without music, in an unbearable continuity, without a return or the approximation of a phrase that approaches and drifts away.

I'm reading Richard Klein, and I think I should celebrate his words by smoking. He's completely right. "Smoking induces forms of aesthetic satisfaction and thoughtful states of consciousness that belong to the most irresistible kinds of artistic and religious experience," he says.

Among my first musical memories is that song by Roque Narvaja with a beautiful refrain. Something like: "I await the morning awake / smoking my time in bed." Back then, at six or seven years old, I was struck by the image of a man smoking time. I think that was when I first associated smoking with the passage of time.

What a good song that was: "Along the streets of my life / I go, mixing truth and lies." I like it when the guy says he's stopped drinking, and now he eats her favorite fruit.

And it's true that I mix, along the streets of my life, truth and lies. As for a favorite fruit, I don't know what mine is. It is absolutely not that disgusting thing that, at first glance, looks like a watermelon, and in Mexico, Colombia, and Ecuador, and I think also in Venezuela, is called a papaya, even though it is nothing like the Chilean papaya. (They say it's the same fruit, but it's hard to believe. And I don't want to look online.) I haven't stopped drinking—I should—but five months ago I stopped smoking, and that has made me into a much healthier and less happy person.

I open the newspaper and mistake the words "Solidarity at Christmas" for "Solitary Christmas." I don't know why they're talking about Christmas, anyway, when it's so far away.

I think that we are heading toward a shitty world where all songs are sung by Diego Torres and all novels are written by Roberto Ampuero. A world where it's better to not even think about dessert, because the only option available is a giant bowl of disgusting rice pudding.

+ + + + +

I'm a correspondent, but I'd like to know of what.

+ + + + +

I don't want the day to come when someone says of me: "He's finished. He doesn't even smoke anymore."
This treatment has been absurd.
I've won a satisfaction that is very false. I should learn how to smoke again.

Seeing as it harms me, I'll never smoke again. But first, I'd like to do it one last time. One more cigarette. A thousand more. I'm only going to smoke a thousand more. The final thousand cigarettes of my life.

I don't know if I'm opening or closing parentheses.
Now:

Part 4

Thank You

I got a feeling you two are together and you're keepin' it a secret"—"No we're not," they answer in unison, and it's the truth: for a little over a month now they've been sleeping together, and they eat, read, and work together, so someone with a tendency to exaggerate, someone who watched them and carefully parsed the words they said to each other, the way their bodies moved closer to each other and entwined— a brash person, someone who still believed in these sorts of things—would say they really loved each other, or that, at least, they felt a dangerous and conspiratorial passion for each other. And yet, they are not together. If there is one thing they are very clear about, it is precisely this: they are not together. She is Argentine and he's Chilean, and it's much better to refer to them like that: the Argentine woman, the Chilean man.

They planned on walking, they talked about how nice it was to go long distances on foot, and they even reached the point where they were dividing people into two groups: those who never walk long distances and those who do—the latter group being, they thought, somehow better. They'd planned on walking, but, on a whim, they hailed a taxi. They had known for months, even before they'd arrived in Mexico

City, when they'd received a set of instructions that was full
of warnings, that they should never hail a taxi in the street,
and up till then it had never occurred to them to hail a taxi
in the street, but this time, on a whim, they did it, and from
the beginning, she thought the driver was going the wrong
way, and she said as much to the Chilean in a whispered
voice, and he reassured her out loud, but his words didn't
even get to take effect because right away the taxi stopped
and two men got in and the Chilean reacted valiantly, reck-
lessly, confusedly, childishly, stupidly: he punched one of the
bandits in the nose, and he went on fighting back for a few,
long seconds while she shouted, "Stop it, stop it, stop it!" The
Chilean stopped, and the bandits let him have it, they showed
him no mercy, they may have even broken something, but
this all happened long ago, a good ten minutes ago now. By
now they've given up their money and their credit cards and
they've recited their ATM PIN numbers and there's only a
little time left—though to them it seems like an eternity—
during which they will ride with their eyes squeezed shut.
"Shut your eyes, pinches cabrones," the two men tell them.

And now there are three men, because the car stopped a
few minutes ago and the taxi driver got out and a third bandit,
who'd been following them in a pickup truck, got behind the
wheel. The new driver hits the Chilean again and feels up the
Argentine, and they accept the punches and the grabbing
hands with a kind of resignation, and wouldn't they like to
know, as we know, that this kidnapping really will be over
soon, that soon they will be walking silently, laboriously,
with their arms around each other, down some street in La
Condesa—because the bandits asked them where they were
going and they replied that they were going to La Condesa

and the bandits said, "Well, we'll drop you off in La Condesa, then. We're not so bad, we don't want to take you too far out of your way," and a second before letting them out, incredibly, the bandits handed them a hundred pesos so they could take a taxi home, but of course they didn't go home by taxi, they got on the subway, and at times she cried and he hugged her tight and at other times he confusedly held back his tears and she moved her feet closer to his the way she had in the taxi, because even though the kidnappers had made them keep their distance, she had kept her right sandal on top of the Chilean's left shoe the whole time.

As so often happens on the Mexico City subway, the train stops for a long time, an inexplicable six or seven minutes, at an intermediate station, and this delay—the type of delay that they are, at this point, very used to—makes them suffer, strikes them as intentional and unnecessary, until eventually the doors close and the train begins to move again, and they finally reach their station and then go on walking together until they reach the house where she lives. Because the Argentine woman and the Chilean man don't live together. He lives with an Ecuadoran writer and she lives with two friends—one Spanish and one Chilean, another Chilean—though they aren't really friends, or they are but that's not why they live together, they are all just passing through, they're all writers and they are in Mexico to write thanks to a grant from the Mexican government, although the thing they do the very least is write, but oddly, when they arrive and open the door, the Spaniard, a very thin and cordial guy with eyes that are maybe a bit too large, is writing, and Chilean

Two isn't there (there's no way around calling him Chilean Two; this story is imperfect because it has two Chileans in it when there should only be one, or even better, much better, none, but there are two). Chilean One and Chilean Two are not friends, either; really they're more like enemies, or at least they were in Chile, and now that they're both in Mexico they are, each in his own way, aware that it would be absurd and unnecessary to go on fighting, and moreover that their fights were tacit ones and nothing was keeping them from trying out a kind of reconciliation, though they also both know that they will never be friends, and that thought is, in a way, a relief. And there is one thing that unites them, in any case: alcohol, since out of the whole group the two of them are, without a doubt, the biggest drinkers.

But Chilean Two isn't there when they come home after the kidnapping, only the Spaniard is there, at the table in the living room, concentrated, writing, beside a bottle of Coke— you could say clinging to a bottle of Coke—but when they tell him what has happened, he puts his work aside and he seems shaken and he comforts them, invites them to talk, eases the mood with a well-timed and lighthearted joke, helps them look for the phone number they need to call to block their credit cards—the thieves took three thousand pesos, two credit cards, two cell phones, two leather jackets, a silver chain, and even a camera. The Chilean had gone back to the apartment to get the camera, he had wanted to take pictures of the Argentine, because she is really beautiful— which is a cliché, but what can you do, the fact is she's beautiful—and of course he has thought about how if he hadn't gone back to get the camera, they wouldn't have taken that particular taxi, the same way so many other things that could have sped them up or slowed them down would have spared them from the kidnapping.

The Argentine and Chilean One tell the Spaniard what happened, and, as they tell him, they relive it, and for the second or third time, they share the experience. Chilean One wonders whether what has just happened is going to bring them closer or drive them apart, and the Argentine wonders exactly the same thing, but neither of them says it out loud. Just then Chilean Two returns. He's coming back from a party, and he sits down to eat a piece of chicken and immediately starts talking without realizing something has happened, but then he sees that Chilean One's face is very swollen and he's holding a bag of ice to it to try to bring the swelling down, and only then does Chilean Two realize—maybe at first it seemed perfectly natural to him that Chilean One would have a bag of ice on his face, maybe in his singular, poet's universe, it is normal for a person to hang out at night with a bag of ice on his face, but no, it's not normal, so Chilean Two asks what happened, and when he finds out he says, "That's horrible, the same thing almost happened to me today," and he sets off talking about the possible attack of which he was almost the victim, but from which he was able to save himself by making a split-second decision to get out of the taxi. While he talks, Chilean One is taking long pulls from a bottle of mescal, and the Spaniard and the Argentine are smoking a joint.

Now someone else arrives, maybe a friend of the Spaniard's, and they go over the whole story once again but focus mostly on the last part, the final half hour in the taxi, which for them is a kind of Part Two, because the kidnapping had lasted an hour, and for the first half of it they feared for their lives, and for the second half they didn't fear for their lives anymore, they were terrified but they vaguely intuited that, however long the kidnapping lasted, the bandits weren't going to kill them, because their words weren't violent anymore, or they *were* violent but in a calm and terrible way: "We've held up Argentines before, but never a Chilean," says the one in the passenger seat, and he sounds truly curious, and he starts to ask Chilean One about the situation in his country, and the Chilean answers politely, as if they were in a restaurant and they were waiter and customer or something, and the guy seems so articulate, so used to that kind of conversation that Chilean One thinks that if he ever tells this story, no one will believe him, and that impression only grows over the next few minutes when the bandit riding with them in the backseat, the one holding the gun, says to them, "I got a feeling you two are together and you're keepin' it a secret," and they respond in unison that no, no they're not. "And why not?" asks the bandit—"Why *aren't* you together? He's not so ugly," he says. "Ugly, but not that ugly, and you'd look better if you cut that hair, it's straight outta the '70s—no one wears their hair like that anymore," he tells the Chilean, "and those giant glasses, too; here, I'm gonna do you a favor," and he takes the glasses off the Chilean's face and throws them out the window. For a second the Chilean thinks about a Woody Allen film he saw recently where the protagonist gets his glasses smashed over and over, and the Chilean smiles slightly, maybe he smiles to himself, he smiles the way we smile in panic, but still, he smiles.

"I can't cut your hair, 'cause we don't have any scissors," the gunman says. "Remind me to bring some good scissors to-morrow so I can cut the Chileans' hair when we hold 'em up, 'cause from now on we're only holding up Chileans. We haven't been very fair: we've held up lots of Argentines but only this one motherfucking Chilean de la chingada, so from now on, we'll specialize in long-haired Chileans. I got a knife, but you can't cut hair with a knife, knives are for cutting off the balls of pinches Chileans. Your boyfriend's got balls, but the ones with balls sometimes gotta lose 'em. Tell your boy-friend not to be so ballsy anymore, 'cause I was just about to wanna fuck you, little Argentine, because of this one's balls, and if I *don't* fuck you, it's not 'cause I'm not into you, you're real hot, of all the Argentine chicks I've ever met, you're the hottest, but I'm working now and when I fuck I'm not work-ing, 'cause if fucking was my job then I'd be a whore, and even though you can't see my face you know I'm no whore, and I wish you could see my face so you'd know I'm one pretty crook who also knows how to cut hair, even though I don't have any scissors and I sure can't cut your hair with this knife, Chilean—I can cut off your dick but you need that to fuck this Argentine hottie, and I can't cut your hair with this gun, either, or maybe I could, but I'd lose the bullets and I need them in case you get your balls back, and then I *would* fuck the Argentine hottie, after I killed you, my Chilean friend, I'd fuck your girlfriend, I didn't plan to kill you but I *would* kill you, and I didn't plan to fuck her but I'd fuck her, because she's really hot, she looks like she's straight outta the best whorehouse in the city. I'd sure choose you, my little Argen-tine, tomorrow I'm gonna get a hooker, and I'll pick the one who looks the most like you, my Argentine hottie."

Then the driver asks the Argentine if she's a Boca fan, and

though it would have been more opportune to say yes, she goes with the truth and says no, she's for Vélez. The Chilean doesn't have this problem, since he's for Colo-Colo, which is the only Chilean team the bandits know. Then they ask about Maradona and the Argentine says something in reply and then the driver comes out with something crazy: he says that Chicharito Hernández is better than Messi, and then he asks them which of Mexico's teams they're for, and the Argentine says she doesn't really know that much about soccer—which is a lie, she knows a lot, she knows much more than that poor robber who thinks Chicharito Hernández is better than Messi—and the Chilean, rather than resorting to a similar lie, gets nervous and thinks hard for a long second about whether the bandits would be for Pumas or for América or Cruz Azul or maybe for Chivas de Guadalajara, since he's heard there are a lot of people in Mexico City who root for Chivas, but in the end he decides to tell the truth and he says that he follows Monterrey because that's who Chupete Suazo plays for, and the driver doesn't like Monterrey but he loves Chupete Suazo and then he says to his companions, "Let's not kill them. In honor of Chupete Suazo we're going to spare their lives."

"Who's Chupete Suazo?" asks Chilean Two, who surely knows but feels obliged to demonstrate that he doesn't care about soccer. Chilean One was going to answer, but the Spaniard knows a lot about soccer and tells Chilean Two that Chupete Suazo is a Chilean center forward who looks fat but isn't, who plays for the Rayados in Monterrey, and who had a successful season when he was lent to Zaragoza, but then went back to Mexico because the Spaniards couldn't afford him. Chilean Two replies that the same thing is true for him, that he's actually skinny but people think he's fat.

Chilean One and the Argentine are still sitting very close together, but they keep a prudent distance, because even though everyone knows or guesses they're together, they still pretend they aren't—not exactly out of propriety, more like desperation, or maybe because the time is gone when things were so simple that you could just be together or not, or maybe everything is still that simple but they've refused to accept it, and it really is absurd that they don't live together because they eat, read, and work together, and, of course, they sleep together—it's almost always him who sleeps over at her place, but sometimes the Argentine stays over at the apartment the Chilean shares with the Ecuadoran girl. What the Chilean and the Argentine really want is to be alone, but the night draws out as they search for new, unremembered details that, once remembered, bring them a new sense of complicity. Finally he says he's going to the bathroom but instead goes into the Argentine's bedroom; she stays a little longer in the living room, and then she also slips away.

She takes a long shower and makes him take one, too, to wash the kidnapping off them, as she says, referring, he assumes, to the groping she'd been subjected to, groping that was certainly not as bad as it could have been, for which they are both thankful. That is, in fact, what she said to the bandits when she got out of the car: "Thank you." She's said it many times over the course of the night: "Thank you, thank you, everyone." To the Spaniard who comforted them, to the Chilean who ignored them but in some way also comforted them, and to the bandits, too, again, it's never a bad idea to repeat it: "Thank you," because you didn't kill us and now life can go on. She also says thank you to Chilean One, as they lie there caressing each other, knowing that tonight they won't make love, that they will spend the hours very close, dangerously, conspiratorially close, talking. Before going to sleep she says thank you to him, and he answers a little late but with conviction: "Thank *you*."

They sleep badly, but they sleep. And they go on talking the next day, as if they had their whole lives in front of them and were willing to work at love, and if someone saw them from outside—someone brash, someone who believed in these kinds of stories, someone who collected them and tried to tell them well, someone who believed in love—he would think that the two of them would be together for a very long time.

The Most Chilean Man in the World

for Gonzalo Maier

In mid-2011 she received a grant from the Chilean government and set off for Leuven to start a doctoral program. He was teaching at a private high school in Santiago, but he wanted to go with her and live some version of "forever." After talking it over, though, at the end of a sad night of very bad sex, they decided it was better to break up.

During the first months, it was hard to tell if Elisa really missed him, even though she sent him all kinds of signals that he thought he interpreted correctly: he was sure that her long emails and the erratic and flirtatious messages on his Facebook wall and, above all, the unforgettable afternoon-nights (afternoons for him, nights for her) of virtual sex via Skype could only be interpreted one way. The natural thing would have been to go on like that for a while and then gradually cool off, forget each other, and maybe, in the best of cases, see each other again someday, maybe many years later, their bodies bearing the weight of other failures, ready now to give it their all. But an executive at Banco Santander, Pedro Aguirre Cerda branch, offered Rodrigo a checking account and credit card, and suddenly he found himself passing from one screen to another, checking boxes that said "yes" and "I agree," entering the codes B4, C9, and F8, and that was how he found himself, at the start of January, without telling anyone—without telling her—on his way to Belgium.

There was no connecting thread, no constant in his thoughts during the nearly twenty-four hours he spent traveling. On the flight to Paris he was surprised at the amount of turbulence, but since he hadn't flown much and certainly never so far, he was, in a way, grateful for the feeling of adventure. He never truly felt afraid, and he even imagined himself saying—oh, so cosmopolitan—that the flight "had been a little rough." He had a couple of books in his backpack, but it was the first time he'd flown on a plane with so many entertainment options, and he spent hours deciding which movies or TV series he wanted to see. In the end he didn't watch anything in its entirety, but he did play, with a degree of skill that surprised him, several rounds of some sort of "Who Wants to Be a Millionaire" game.

While he was walking through Charles de Gaulle to take the train, he had the fairly conventional thought that no, he did not want to be a millionaire, he'd never wanted to be a millionaire. And that trivial thought led him, who knows how, to a scorned and maligned word, which nevertheless now glittered, or at least shone a little, or was less dark than usual, or was dark and serious and big but didn't embarrass him: maturity. He went on thinking about this on the train ride from Brussels to Leuven. Inexplicably, using up almost all of the credit on his card to buy a plane ticket to Europe to visit Elisa struck him as a sign of maturity.

And what happened in Leuven? The worst. Although sometimes the worst is the best thing that can happen. It must be said that Elisa could have been nicer, a little less cruel. But if she had been nicer, he might not have understood. She didn't want to leave that possibility open. He called her from the station, and Elisa thought it was a joke but started walking toward him anyway, talking to him on the phone all the while. Then she turned a corner and saw him, a hundred steps away, but she didn't tell him she was there and he went right on talking, sitting on his suitcase, half numb and anxious, looking at the ground and then at the sky with a mixture of confidence and naivete that Elisa found repulsive—she couldn't put her feelings, her thoughts, in order, but she was sure of one thing: she didn't want to spend the coming days with Rodrigo, not those days or any others, none. And maybe she was still a little in love, maybe she cared about him and liked to talk to him, but for him to show up out of nowhere like in some bad movie, ready to embrace and be embraced, ready to become the star, the hero who crossed the world for love: that was, for Elisa, much more of an affront and a humiliation than a cause for happiness.

As she took long strides back to her house, she felt the constant vibration of her cell phone in her pocket, but she only answered half an hour later, already in bed, duly protected: "I'm not going to pick you up," she told him. "I don't want to see you. I have a boyfriend [lie]. I live with him. I don't ever want to see you ever again." There were another nine calls, and all nine times she answered and said more or less the same thing, and in the end she told him, to give the thing a little realism, that her boyfriend was German.

Of course there are other reasons for her reaction, there's another story that runs parallel to this one, one that explains why Elisa didn't ever want to see Rodrigo again: a story that talks about the need for a real change, the need to leave behind her small Chilean world of Catholic school, her desire to seek out other paths, a story that explains why, in the end, it was logical and even healthy to break up with Rodrigo definitively—maybe not like that, maybe it wasn't fair of her to leave him sitting there, pining and numb, but she had to break it off with him. In any case, for now, she is stretched out on her bed, listening to some album that falls somewhere on the broad spectrum of alternative music (the latest from Beach House, for example), and she feels at ease.

Rodrigo ventures out on a quick and disoriented walk around the city. He sees twenty or thirty women who all look more beautiful than Elisa; he wonders why Hans—he decides the German's name is Hans—chose Elisa, a Chilean who isn't even all that voluptuous or dark-skinned, and then he remembers how good she is in bed, and he feels rotten. He goes on walking, though now all he sees is a beautiful city full of beautiful people, and he thinks what a whore Elisa is, and other things typical of a scorned man. He walks aimlessly, but Leuven is too small a city to walk around aimlessly in, and after a little while he is back at the station. He stops in front of the Fonske, which is practically the only thing Elisa had mentioned about the city: that there is a fountain with the statue of a boy (or a student or a man) who is looking at the formula for happiness in a book and pouring water (or beer) over his head. The fountain strikes him as strange, even aggressive or grotesque, and he tries to avoid engaging with the irony of a "formula for happiness." He goes on looking at the fountain—which for some reason that day is turned off and dry—while he smokes a cigarette, the first since he's been off the train, the first on European soil, a pilgrim Belmont cigarette from Chile. And although during all this time he has felt an intense cold, only now does he feel the urgency of the freezing wind on his face and body, as if the cold was really trying to work its way into his bones. He opens his suitcase, finds a pair of loose-fitting pants, and puts them on over the ones he is wearing, along with another shirt, an extra pair of socks, and a knit cap (he doesn't have gloves). For a moment, carried along by rage and a sense of drama, he thinks that he is going to die of cold, literally. And that this is ironic, because Elisa had always been the more cold-natured one; she was always cold, more than any other girlfriend he'd had, more than any other woman he'd met: even during the summer, at night, she used to wear jackets and shawls and sleep with a hot-water bottle.

Sitting near the station, in front of a small waffle shop, he remembers the joke about the most cold-blooded man in the world, the only joke his father ever used to tell. He remembers his dad beside the bonfire, on the wide-open beach at Pelluhue, many years ago: he was a distant and taciturn man, but when he told that joke, he became another person, every sentence coming out of his mouth as though spurred by some mysterious mechanism, and upon seeing him like that—wisely setting up his audience, preparing for the imminent peals of laughter—one might think that he was a funny and witty man, maybe a specialist in telling these kinds of shaggy-dog jokes, which can be told so many different ways, because the important thing isn't the punch line, but rather the flair of the teller, his feeling for detail, his ability to fill the air with digressions without losing the audience's interest. The joke started in Punta Arenas, with a baby crying from cold and his parents desperately wrapping him up in wool blankets from Chiloé. Then, surrendering to the obvious, they decide they must find a better climate for the baby, and they start to climb up the map of Chile in search of the sun. They go from Concepción to Talca, to Curicó, to San Fernando, always heading north, passing through Santiago and, after a lot of adventures, heading up to La Serena and Antofagasta, until finally they reach Arica, the so-called city of eternal spring, but it's no use: the boy, who by now is a teenager, still feels cold. As an adult, the coldest man in the world travels through Latin America in search of a more favorable clime, but he never—not in Iquitos or Guayaquil or Maracaibo or Mexicali or Rio de Janeiro—stops feeling a profound and lacerating cold.

He feels it in Arizona, in California, and he arrives and departs from Cairo and Tunis wrapped in blankets, shivering, convulsing, complaining interminably, but in a nice way, because, in spite of what a bad a time of it he had, the coldest man in the world always remained polite and cordial, and perhaps because of this, when the much-feared ending finally came—when the coldest man in the world, who was Chilean, finally died of cold—no one doubted that he would go directly, without any major trouble, to Heaven.

Cairo, Arizona, Tunis, California, thinks Rodrigo, almost

smiling: Leuven. It's been months since he's seen his father—they've grown apart after some stupid argument. He thinks that, in a situation like this one, his father would want him to be brave. No, actually he doesn't know what his father would think about a situation like the one he is in. His father would never have a credit card, much less irresponsibly travel thousands of miles to be given the kind of kick in the stomach that his son has just received. What would my dad do in this situation? Rodrigo wonders again, earnestly. He doesn't know. Maybe he should go straight back to Chile. Or maybe he should stay in Belgium for good, make a life here—why not? He decides, for the moment, to go back to Brussels.

People travel from Leuven to Brussels, or from Brussels to Antwerp, or from Antwerp to Ghent, but they are such short journeys that it's almost excessive to consider them travel in the proper sense of the word. And even so, to Rodrigo, the half hour to Brussels seems like an eternity. He thinks about Elisa and Hans walking around that city, such a university town, so European and correct. Again he remembers Elisa's body: he recalls her convalescing after she had her appendix out, greeting him with a sweet, pained smile. And he remembers her some time later, one Sunday morning, completely naked, massaging rose-hip oil into the scar. And later, maybe that same Sunday night, playing with the warm semen around that scar, drawing something like letters with her index finger, excited and laughing hard.

He gets off the train and walks a few blocks, but he doesn't look at the city, he goes on thinking about Elisa, about Hans, about Leuven, and nearly forty minutes go by before he realizes he has forgotten his suitcase on the train. He left it in a corner next to the other passengers' luggage and got off carrying only his backpack. He says to himself, out loud, emphatically: "Asshole."

He buys some French fries near the station and sits down on a corner to eat. When he stands up again he feels dizzy, or something like dizziness. He was planning on buying cigarettes and then walking for a while, but he has to stop because of this feeling, which just seems like a nuisance at first, an impression of vertigo that he has never felt before, but which immediately starts to grow, as if freeing itself from something, and soon he feels that he is going to fall, but he manages, with a lot of effort, to maintain the minimum stability necessary to move forward. The backpack weighs next to nothing, but he puts it down and takes five steps forward and back, to test himself. The dizziness continues, and he has to stop completely and lean against the window of a shoe store. He walks forward slowly, his hands moving along one shop window after another like Spider-Man's cowardly apprentice, while he looks out of the corner of his eye at the interiors of the stores overflowing with different kinds of chocolates, beers, and lamps, some of them selling strange gifts: drumsticks that are also chopsticks, a mug in the shape of a camera lens, an endless array of figurines.

An hour later he has only made it seven blocks, but fortunately, at a kiosk, he finds a blue umbrella that costs him ten euros. At first he still feels unstable when he walks, but the umbrella gives him confidence, and after a few steps, he feels like he's gotten used to the wobbling. Only then does he look at or focus on the city; only then does he try to understand it, start to understand it. He thinks it's all a dream, that he's near Plaza de Armas, near the Cathedral, in the Peruvian neighborhood of Santiago de Chile. No, he doesn't think that: he thinks that he thinks he's in Plaza de Armas. He thinks that he thinks it's all a dream.

The stores are starting to close. It's hard to know if it's day or night: 5:15 p.m., and the lights of apartments and cars are already on. He starts to walk away from downtown, then instinctively goes into a laundromat and decides to stay there for a while—he doesn't really decide, actually, but that is where he stays, along with two guys who are reading while they wait for their clothes. It isn't exactly warm in there, but at least it isn't cold. It's absurd—he knows that he's short on money, that he's going to need every cent—but still, he removes one of the pairs of pants, the second shirt, and the extra pair of socks, and it takes him a while to figure out how the washing machine works—it's old and looks sort of dangerous—but he feels a stupid and absolute satisfaction once it starts humming. He sits there looking at the tumbling clothes, entranced or paralyzed, focused like someone watching the end of a championship game on TV, and maybe for him this is even more interesting than the end of a championship game, because while he's watching the tumbling clothes pushed up against the glass, soaked in soapy water, he thinks, as if discovering something important, how these clothes are his, how they belong to him, how he has worn those pants a hundred times, those socks, too, and how once upon a time that shirt, a little faded now, was his best, the one he preferred on special occasions. He remembers his own body sporting that shirt with pride, and it's a strange vision, vain and awkward. It is perhaps his kitsch idea of purification.

Then he goes into a pizzeria called Bella Vita, which looks cheap. He's waited on by Bülent, a very friendly and cheerful Turkish man who speaks some French and a little Flemish but no English, so they have to communicate exclusively through gestures and a reciprocal murmur that perhaps only serves to demonstrate that neither of them is mute. He eats a Neapolitan pizza that tastes out of this world to him, and then sits there sipping his coffee. He doesn't know what to do, he doesn't want to go on wandering, but he can't make up his mind to look for a cheap hotel or a hostel. He tries to ask Bülent if the place has wifi, but it is truly difficult to mime the idea of wifi, and at this point he is so helpless that he doesn't think of the simplest option, which would have been to say "wifi" and pronounce it in all possible ways until Bülent understood. Luckily Piet comes in just then; he's a very tall guy who wears glasses with thick, red rims and has an unspecifiable number of piercings in his right eyebrow. Piet knows English and a little Spanish—he has even been to Chile, for a month, years ago. Rodrigo finally has someone to talk to.

A couple of hours later they are in the living room of Piet's beautiful apartment across from the pizzeria. While his host makes coffee, Rodrigo watches from the window as Bülent, with the help of the waitress and another man, closes the place up for the night. Rodrigo feels something like the pulse or the pain or the aura of daily life. He turns on his laptop and connects to the internet; there are no messages from Elisa, but he wasn't really expecting any. He tries to find a friend from high school who, as he remembers it, has lived in Brussels for several years. He tracks him down easily on Facebook, and the friend responds right away but says that he's in Chile now taking care of his sick mother, and although he plans to come back to university, for now he's in Santiago indefinitely. Ten minutes later Rodrigo gets another message, in which the friend recommends that he not be afraid to drink *peket* ("It's a good buzz, but a bad hangover"), that he avoid the grilled endive ("no to the grilled endive, yes to the *boulettes de viande* and to the *moules et frites*"), that he try the hot dogs with warm sauerkraut and mustard, that he buy chocolates at Galler, near the Grand-Place, that he go to the Tropismes bookstore, and that he shouldn't miss the Music Museum or the Magritte Museum—all details that seem remote to Rodrigo, almost impossible, because this isn't a vacation, it never was. He feels desperate. He doesn't have much credit left on his card, and he only has a hundred euros in his wallet.

That's when Bart arrives, Piet's editor, who lives in Utrecht. Only then does Rodrigo find out that Piet is a writer, that he has published two books of short stories and a novel. He appreciates Piet's discretion, his modesty. He thinks that if he were a writer, he wouldn't go around proclaiming it to the world, either.

Bart is almost six and a half feet tall, even more of a giant than Piet. Along with a friend, who is also named Bart, he runs a small press that publishes emerging writers, almost all of them fiction writers, almost all of them Dutch, but a few Belgians, too. The other Bart, oddly, lives in Colombia (he fell in love with a woman from Popayán, Rodrigo learns), but he handles everything online from there. This Bart's job is to manage distribution—to a series of small bookstores, none of them chains—and organize intimate events and conferences where he sells the books himself.

Bart is friendly and tells his story in pretty fluent English,

although he is helped by his emphatic gestures and a certain
talent for mimicry when words fail him. It's almost ten;
they walk for a few blocks. Rodrigo feels better. He leans on
the umbrella cane, but more out of precaution than necessity.
They reach La Vesa, a somewhat gloomy bar that has poetry readings on Thursdays, but today isn't Thursday, it's
Tuesday, and patrons are scarce, which is better, thinks Rodrigo, who enjoys this feeling of intimacy, of routine camaraderie, this sensible chatting with new friends, and the brief,
ironic comments interjected occasionally by Laura, an Italian
waitress who isn't beautiful at first glance, but who becomes
beautiful as the minutes pass, not from the effect of the alcohol, but because you have to look at her really closely to discover her beauty. His friends are drinking Orval, and Rodrigo
orders wine by the glass; Piet asks him if he dislikes beer,
and he replies that he likes it, but he's still too cold and he
prefers the warmth of wine. They start talking about Belgian
beer, which is the best in the world. Piet tells him it's not so
cold out, that there have been many worse winters. Then Rodrigo wants to tell them the joke about the coldest man in
the world, but he doesn't know how to say *friolento*, "cold-
natured," in English, so he says "I am" and makes the gesture
of shivering, and Bart tells him "You're chilly," and it all gets
tangled up because Rodrigo thinks they're talking about
Chile, about whether he's from Chile, which supposedly they
already knew, until, after several misunderstandings that
they celebrate thunderously, they understand that the joke is
about the chilliest man on earth, and Rodrigo adds that the
most cold-blooded man on earth is definitely Chilean, he's
the chilliest man on earth, and he laughs heartily, for the first

time he laughs on Belgian soil the way he would laugh on Chilean soil.

Rodrigo starts the joke uncertainly, because as he strings the story together, he thinks that maybe in Belgium and Holland they have the same joke, that maybe there are as many versions of the joke as there are countries in the world. His listeners react well, however, giving themselves over to the story: they enjoy the enumeration of the cities whose names sound so strange to them ("Arica sounds like Osaka," says Bart), and when the chilliest man in the world, who was Chilean, dies of cold under the burning sun of Bangkok, his friends let out a nervous giggle and grab their heads in a mournful gesture.

The chilliest man in the world had been a good son, a good father, a good Christian, so Saint Peter accepts him into Heaven without delay, but the problems start immediately: incredibly, even though in Heaven hot and cold don't exist—at least not in the way we understand them down here—and even though all the rooms in the formidable hotel that is Heaven automatically adjust to the needs of their guests, the Chilean still feels cold, and in his friendly but also very persistent manner he goes right on complaining, until the blessed patience that reigns in Heaven runs out, everyone gets fed up, and they all agree that the chilliest man in the world should go find a truly beneficial climate. It is God himself who decides to send him to Hell, where it's unthinkable that he could go on feeling cold. But in spite of the unquenchable fires, the frightful burning seas, the colossal hot-water bottles, and the human heat, which gets pretty intense in such an overcrowded place, the chilliest man in the world still feels cold, and the case becomes so famous that it reaches the ears of Satan, who sees it as a fun challenge and decides to take matters into his own hands.

One morning, Satan himself leads the Chilean to nothing less than the hottest place imaginable: the center of the sun. It's so hot there that Satan has to put on a special suit or else he'll get burned. Once inside the center of the sun, they come to a small, two-by-two-meter cubicle, and Satan opens the door. The Chilean enters and stays there, hopeful and deeply grateful. Weeks pass, months, years, until one day, moved by curiosity, the Devil decides to pay the Chilean a visit. He puts on his special suit again—even reinforces it with two additional layers, because he thinks he may have singed himself on the previous trip—and he heads off to the sun. He has scarcely opened the door to the cubicle when he hears the Chilean shout from inside: "Please close the door, it's chilly in here!"

"Please close the door, it's chilly in here!" says Rodrigo, and his performance is a success.

"I think that you are the chilliest man in the world," Bart tells him, "and I want the chilliest man in the world to try the best beer in the world." Piet proposes they go to a bar where they sell hundreds of beers, but in the end they decide to go somewhere closer, to a bar that covertly sells Westvleteren, the so-called best beer in the world, and on the way Rodrigo leans on the umbrella, but he's not sure if it's necessary, he feels like he doesn't need it anymore and could throw it away, but he goes on using it anyway while he listens to the story of the Trappist monks who make the beer and sell it only in judicious quantities, a story he finds amazing; he hopes he likes the beer a lot, and he does, though they only buy one for the three of them, because the bottle costs ten euros.

They go back to the apartment at two in the morning with their arms around one another, so Rodrigo doesn't have to use the umbrella: they look drunker than they are. Later, in the living room, they go on drinking for a while, they half listen to each other, they laugh. "You can stay, but only for tonight," says Piet, and Rodrigo thanks him. They drag in a mattress while Bart stretches out on an old chaise longue and covers himself with a blanket. Rodrigo thinks about what he will do if Bart tries something in the middle of the night. He considers whether he will reject him or not, but he falls asleep, and Bart does, too.

He wakes up early; he's alone in the living room. He's a little hungover, and the coffee he finds in the kitchen does him good. He looks at the street, at the buildings, the silent facade of the pizzeria. He wants to say goodbye to Piet, and he cracks open the door to his room: he sees him sleeping next to Bart in a half embrace. He leaves them a note of thanks and goes down the four flights of stairs. He has absolutely no plan, but he's encouraged by the idea of walking without a cane, and once in the street he tries it, like in a happy ending. But he can't do it, and he falls. It's a nasty fall, a hard fall, his double pants rip, his knee bleeds. He stays on the corner, thinking, paralyzed by pain, and it starts to rain, as if he were a cartoon character with a cloud hanging above him—but this rain is for everyone, not just him.

It's a cold and copious rain, and he should look for shelter. He has very little money left, but he has no choice but to buy another umbrella. This is the moment to think of Elisa and curse her, but he doesn't do it. Now he has two umbrellas, a blue one for balance and a black one for the rain; he says it out loud, with the same calm tone in which he would say his name, first and last, and his birthplace. "Now I have two umbrellas, blue for balance and black for rain," he repeats, as he starts to walk, with no other purpose than that, simply: to walk.

Family Life

for Paula Canal

It's not hot out, it's not cold. A shy and clear sun overcomes the clouds, and the sky looks, at times, truly clean, like the sky blue of a child's drawing. Martín is in the last seat of the bus, listening to music, bobbing his head like a teenager. But he's not young anymore, not by a long shot: he's forty years old, his hair fairly long, black, and a little curly, his face extremely white—well, there'll be time for descriptions later. Right now he has just gotten off the bus carrying a backpack and a suitcase, and he is walking a few blocks in search of an address.

The job consists of taking care of the cat, running the vacuum cleaner every once in a while, and watering some indoor plants that seem destined to dry out. I'm not going to go out much, hardly at all, he thinks, with a hint of happiness. Only to buy food for the cat, and food for myself. There is also a silver Fiat that he has to drive every so often ("so it can breathe," they've told him). For now, he's spending time with the family: it's seven in the evening, and they'll be leaving very early, at 5:30 a.m. Here is the family, in alphabetical order:

> —Bruno—sparse beard, blondish, tall, smoker of black tobacco, professor of literature.

> —Consuelo—Bruno's partner, not his wife, because they never married, although they act like a married couple, perhaps worse than a married couple.

> —Sofía, their daughter.

She's just run past, the little girl, chasing the cat toward the stairs. She doesn't greet Martín, doesn't look at him; these days kids don't say hi, and maybe that's not such a bad thing, because adults greet each other too much. Bruno explains some of the details of the job to Martín, while at the same time arguing with Consuelo about how to organize a suitcase. Then Consuelo approaches Martín with a warmth that unsettles him, because he isn't used to warmth. She shows him the cat's bed, the litter box, and a piece of pressed cloth where the cat can sharpen its claws—although none of them get much use, according to Consuelo, because the cat sleeps wherever he feels like it, does his business in the yard, and scratches all the furniture. Consuelo also shows him how the pet door works, the mechanism that allows the cat to go out but not come in, or come in but not go out, or come in or out as he pleases—"We always leave it open," says Consuelo, "so he can be free—it's like when our parents finally gave us the keys to the house."

To Martín, the existence of that door is fantastic—he's

only ever seen one like it in Tom and Jerry cartoons. He almost asks how they got it, but then he thinks that maybe Santiago is full of pet doors and he's just never noticed them before.

"Sorry," he says, returning to the conversation: "What was that about our parents?"

"What?"

"You said something about 'our parents,' I think?"

"Oh, just that this door is like when our parents gave us the keys to the house."

The laughter lasts for two seconds. Martín goes out to smoke and sees an empty area in the yard: two and a half meters of disheveled grass where there should be a few plants and maybe a bush, but there's nothing. He flicks his ashes furtively onto the grass, puts out the cigarette, and wastes an entire minute thinking about where to throw it: in the end he leaves it under a yellowed weed. He looks at the house from the threshold, thinks that it isn't so big, that it's manageable, though it seems full of nuance. He tentatively observes the shelves, the electric piano, and a large hourglass on the end table. He remembers that when he was a child he liked hourglasses, and he turns it over—

"It lasts twelve minutes," says the little girl, who then, from the top step where she is trying to hold on to the cat, asks him if he's Martín.

"Yes."

And if he wants to play chess.

"Okay."

The cat wriggles out of the girl's grasp. It's an uneven gray color, with short, dense fur, a thin body, and fangs that protrude slightly. Sofía goes up and down the stairs several times. And the cat, Mississippi, seems docile. He approaches Martín, who wants to pet him but hesitates: he's not so familiar with cats, he's never lived with one before.

Sofia comes back, now in her PJs and walking clumsily in big Chilote slippers. Consuelo asks her to not bother them and to go to her room, but the girl is carrying a heavy box, or a box that's heavy for her, and she sets up the chessboard on the living room table. She is seven years old and has just learned how to move the pieces, as well as the game's mannerisms or affectations: she looks cute with her brow furrowed, her round face in her hands. She and Martín start to play, but after five minutes it's clear that they're getting bored, him more so than her. Then he proposes to Sofi that they play at losing, and at first she doesn't understand, but then she explodes in sweet and mocking laughter—the one who loses wins, the goal is to give up first, to leave Don Quixote and Dulcinea unprotected, because it's a Cervantes chess set, with windmills instead of rooks, and earnest Sancho Panzas as pawns.

How idiotic, thinks Martín, a literary chess set.

The pieces on the board look tarnished, tasteless, and although he's not one to form quick impressions, the whole house now makes him a little anxious and annoyed, but not because of anything he sees: the placement of each object surely answers to some obscure theory of interior design, but an imbalance persists nonetheless, a secret anomaly. It's as if the things don't want to be where they are, thinks Martín, who is still grateful for the chance to spend some time in this luminous house, so different from the small, shadowy rooms he tends to live in.

Consuelo takes Sofi upstairs and sings her to sleep. Though he can't help hearing, Martín feels like he shouldn't be eavesdropping, like he is an intruder. Bruno offers him some ravioli, which they eat in silence with a phony masculine voracity. Something like, Well, there are no women around—let's not use napkins. After the coffee, Bruno pours a couple of vodkas on the rocks, but Martín opts to keep downing the wine.

"What's the name of the city where you're going to live?" asks Martín, to have something to say.

"Saint-Étienne."

"Where we played?"

"Who's we?"

"The Chilean soccer team, France, '98."

"I don't know. It's an industrial city, a little run-down. I'm going to teach classes on Latin America."

"And where is it?"

"Saint-Étienne or Latin America?"

The joke is so easy, so rote, but it works. Almost without trying, they draw out the after-dinner conversation, as if discovering some belated affinity. Upstairs, Sofi is asleep, and they can also hear what might be Consuelo breathing or snoring slightly. Martín discovers that he has been thinking about her the whole time he's been in the house, from the moment he saw her in the doorway.

"You're going to be here four months," Bruno tells him.

"Make use of that time to have a go with one of the neigh-bors."

I'd much rather have a go with your wife, thinks Martín, and he thinks it so forcefully he's afraid he has said it out loud.

"Enjoy it, cousin," Bruno goes on affectionately, slightly drunk. They aren't first cousins, their fathers were: Martín's has just died, and it was at the wake that they saw each other again for the first time in years. To treat one another like family now makes sense, it's perhaps the only way to build a hasty sense of trust. The idea had originally been to rent out the house, but only to subletters who wouldn't change the place too much. They couldn't find anyone. After a lot of searching they were pretty near desperate, and Martín was the most reliable person Bruno could find to house-sit. They've seen each other very little over the course of their lives, but maybe they were friends at one point, when they were children and were compelled to play together on some Sunday afternoon.

Bruno lays out for him again what they've already talked about over the phone. He gives him the keys, they test the locks, he explains the doors' quirks. And again he lists the advantages of being there, although now he doesn't mention any neighbors. Then he asks if Martín likes to read.

"A little," says Martín, but it's not true. Then he turns overly honest: "No, I don't like to read. The last thing I would ever do is read a book." After a pause he says, "Sorry," and glances at the overflowing shelves: "It's like I've gone to church and said I don't believe in God. Plus, there are lots of things that are worse. Even worse than the things that've already happened to me." He gives Bruno a placating smile.

"Don't worry about it," Bruno says, as if approving the comment. "A lot of people feel that way, they just don't say it." Then he picks out some novels and puts them on the end table beside the hourglass. "Still, if you ever do feel like reading, here are some things that might interest you."

"Why would they interest me? Are they for people who don't read?"

"More or less, ha" (he says this, "ha," but without the inflection of laughter). "Some of them are classics, others are more contemporary, but they're all entertaining." (When he says this last word, he doesn't make the slightest effort to avoid the pedantic tone, almost as if he were making air quotes.) Martín thanks him and says good night.

Martín doesn't look at the books, not even their titles. Lying on the couch, he thinks: Books for people who don't read. He thinks: Books for people who have just lost their fathers and had already lost their mothers, people who are alone in the world. Books for people who have failed at university, at work, at love (he thinks this: failed at love). Books for people who have failed so badly that, at forty years old, taking care of someone else's house in exchange for nothing, or almost nothing, seems like a good opportunity. Some people count sheep, others recite their misfortunes. But he doesn't sleep, he has sunk too deep into self-pity, which, in spite of everything, is not a suit he is comfortable wearing.

Just when he's about to drop off, the alarm clocks go off; it's five in the morning. Martín gets up to help the family with their suitcases. Sofi comes downstairs sulking but very soon switches on a hidden reserve of energy. Mississippi is nowhere to be found, and Sofi wants to say goodbye. She cries for two minutes but then stops, as if she had simply forgotten she was crying. When the taxi arrives she insists she wants to finish her cereal, but then leaves the bowl almost untouched.

"Kill all the robbers," she tells Martín before climbing into the car.

"And what should I do with the ghosts?"

"Martín is joking." Consuelo jumps in, throwing him a nervous look. "There are no ghosts in the house—that's why we bought it, because we were guaranteed there were no ghosts. And not in France, either, in the house where we're going to live."

As soon as they are gone, Martín stretches out in the big bed, which is still warm. He searches in the sheets for Consuelo's perfume or the smell of her body, and he sleeps face-down, breathing deeply into the pillow as if he's discovered an exclusive and dangerous drug. The noise of the street starts up, the commotion of people going to work, the school buses, engines revved by drivers anxious to beat the traffic. He dreams that he is in the waiting room of a hospital and a stranger asks him if he's gotten his results yet. Dream-Martín is waiting for something or for someone, but he doesn't remember exactly what or who, and he doesn't dare ask, he just knows that what he's waiting for isn't test results. He tries to remember, and then he thinks, It's a dream, and he tries to wake up, but when he wakes he is still in the dream and the stranger is still waiting for an answer. Then he wakes up for real and feels the immense relief of not having to answer that question, of not having to answer any questions. The cat yawns at the foot of the bed.

He unpacks his suitcase in the master bedroom, but there's not much room in the wardrobes. There are several plastic bags and boxes full of clothes meticulously packed up, but there are also some unboxed garments. He finds an old Pixies T-shirt with the cover from *Surfer Rosa*. "You'll think I'm dead, but I'll sail away," he thinks—right, that's from a different album, he's got it wrong. He tries to picture Consuelo in that shirt and he can't, but it's a medium, so it must be hers and not Bruno's. In any case, he puts it on—it's too tight on him, and he looks funny. Wearing only the T-shirt and a pair of sweatpants, he heads out to the nearest supermarket, where he buys coffee, beer, noodles, and ketchup, plus some cans of mackerel for Mississippi, because he's hatched a diabolical plan, thinking the cat will see the situation like this: They're gone, they left me alone with a stranger, but I sure am eating great. He comes back practically dragging the bags: it's several blocks away, and he knows he should have taken the car, but he's terrified of driving. Back in the house, as he's putting away the groceries in the kitchen, he looks at the cereal and milk that Sofi left behind. He finishes what's left in the bowl while thinking that he can count on one hand the times he's eaten cereal. Men from my generation don't eat cereal, he thinks—unless their children eat it, unless they are fathers. When did they start selling cereal in Chile? The nineties? Suddenly, this question seems important. He sees an image of himself as a child, drinking a glass of plain milk, like he always did, and then rushing off to school.

Afterward, he inspects the second floor, where Bruno has his study—a large room, perfectly illuminated by a skylight, with books in strict alphabetical order, countless office supplies, and degrees on the wall: undergraduate, master's, doctorate, all hanging in a line. Next he takes a look at Sofi's room, full of drawings, decorations, and, on the bed, some stuffed animals with their names written on tags. She'd taken some of her animals with her, and others were stored away in her closet or toy chest, but she'd left five out on her bed and insisted on giving them name tags so Martín could identify them (one brown bear in workout gear catches his attention—its name is Dog). Then he finds, in a pile of magazines in the upstairs bathroom, a booklet of sheet music for beginners. He goes downstairs and sits at the electric piano, which doesn't work; he tries to fix it, with no luck. Still, he reads the music and presses the keys. He has fun imagining that he is an impoverished piano player, one with no money to pay the electricity bill and who has to practice every day like this, by touch.

The first two weeks pass uneventfully. He lives just as he had planned. At first the days seem eternal, but gradually he fills them with certain routines: he gets up at nine, feeds Mississippi, and, after breakfast (he goes on eating cereal after discovering a love for Quaker Oatmeal Squares), he goes into the garage, starts the car's engine, and plays a bit with the accelerator, like a pilot waiting for the signal to take off. At first he moves the car timidly, but then dares to take it out for a spin, for multiple spins, each one longer than the last. When he comes back, he tunes the radio to the news, opens the window in the living room, and turns the hourglass upside down; while the grains, the minutes, fall delicately and decisively, he smokes the day's first cigarette.

Then he watches TV for a few hours, and the effect is narcotic. He comes to feel affection for the rhetoric of the morning shows, of which he becomes something of a scholar; he compares them, considers them seriously, and he does the same with the celebrity shows. Those take a bit more effort, because he doesn't know the characters—he's never paid attention to that world—but eventually he comes to recognize them. He eats his lunch of noodles with ketchup in bed, always watching TV.

The rest of the day is uncertain, but it tends to be spent walking. He has a rule not to go to the same café twice or buy his cigarettes from the same corner shop, in order to avoid building any sense of familiarity: he has the vague impression that he is going to miss this life, which isn't the life he's dreamed of, but is a good life nonetheless; it is a beneficial, restorative time. But all of that changes the day he discovers that the cat has disappeared. It's been at least two days since he's seen Mississippi, and the bowl of food is untouched. He asks around with the neighbors: no one knows anything.

For several hours he is desperate, paralyzed, he doesn't know what to do. In the end he decides to make a flyer. He searches on the computer erratically, incoherently, for a photo of Mississippi, but he finds nothing; before leaving, Bruno had cleared all personal files from the hard drive. Distraught,

Martín ransacks the entire house, taking a certain pleasure in the disarray, the chaos he is sowing. He searches carelessly through trunks, bags, and boxes, dozens of books, flipping frenetically through the pages, or shaking them with something like rage. He finds a little red case hidden in the wardrobe of the study. Instead of money or jewelry it holds hundreds of family photos, some of them framed and others loose, with dates on the back of them and even some short, loving messages. He likes one photo in particular, a large one in which Consuelo poses, blushing, with her mouth open. He takes a certificate Sofi received from a swimming course out of its frame and replaces it with the photo of Consuelo, and then he hangs the photo on the main wall of the living room. He thinks that he could spend hours stroking that straight, shiny black hair. Since he couldn't find any photos of Mississippi, he searches online for images of gray cats and chooses one at random. He writes a brief message, prints some forty copies, and puts them up on lampposts and trees all along the street.

When he comes back, the house is a disaster, especially the second floor. Now he is annoyed at being the author of that mess. He looks at the half-opened boxes, the clothes strewn across the bed, the many dolls, drawings, and bracelets scattered over the floor, the solitary Lego blocks lost in corners. He thinks that he has profaned the space. He feels like a thief or a cop, and he even thinks of that horrible, exaggerated word: raid. Reluctantly, he starts to straighten up the room, but suddenly he stops, lights a cigarette, and blows some smoke rings like he used to do as a teenager, all while imagining that Sofi has just been playing here with her friends. He imagines himself as the father who opens her door and indignantly demands she clean up her room, and she nods but keeps right on playing. He imagines going into the living room, where a very beautiful woman, a woman who is Consuelo, or who looks like Consuelo, hands him a mug of coffee, raises her eyebrows, and smiles, showing her teeth. Then he goes to the living room and makes that cup of coffee for himself, which he drinks in quick sips while he thinks about a life with children, a wife, a stable job. Martín feels a sharp jab in his chest. And then a word that was by now inevitable looms and conquers: melancholy.

He contents or distracts himself with the memory that he, too, long ago, had been the father of a girl the same age, seven years old. For a day, at least. He was nineteen then and lived in Recoleta with his father and mother, neither of whom had gotten sick yet. One day, he went down to the kitchen and overheard Elba, the woman who helped around the house, complaining because she could never go to the parents' meetings at her daughter's school. He offered to go in her place, because he cared about Elba and Cami, but also out of his sense of adventure, which, back then, was very pronounced. He had long hair and looked very young—in no way did he look like a father—but he went into the school and sat at the back of the room next to a guy who was almost as young as him, though a little more of a man, as they say, a little more worldly.

On his right arm the man had a brown tattoo that was barely darker than his skin. It said: *Jesús*.

"What's your name?" Martín asked the man. He responded by indicating the tattoo. Jesús seems nice, Martín thought.

"You look really young," he told Martín.

"You, too."

"I was still a kid when I had my kid." Just then the teacher closed the door and started to talk; some parents came in late and the door got stuck, once, twice. No one said anything until a fat blond woman in the third row got up, and with an enviably resounding voice, interrupted the teacher: "How can this be, what would happen if there was an earthquake or a fire, what would happen to the children?"

The teacher fell into the silence of one who knows she should think carefully about what she is going to say. It was precisely the moment when she could have blamed her bosses, the system, the municipalization of public education, Pinochet, the ineffectiveness of the Concertación party, capitalism. It was clearly not the teacher's fault, but she didn't think fast enough, she wasn't brave: the voices accumulated and she let them build, everyone was complaining, everyone was shouting, and to make matters worse, right then someone else arrived late and the door jammed again. Jesús was shouting and even Martín was about to join in, but the teacher asked them to show some respect and let her talk: "I'm sorry, this is a poor school, we just don't have the resources. I understand you are angry, but keep in mind that if there is a fire or an earthquake, I'll also be trapped in here with the children." The effect of this grim observation lasted two or three seconds, until Martín got up furiously and pointed his finger at her and said, leaning into the dramatics: "But you, ma'am, are not my daughter!" Everyone supported him, enraged, and he felt so good about himself.

"That was rad," said Jesús later, congratulating him on the way to the bus. As they said goodbye, Martín asked if he believed in Jesus. And Jesús responded with a smile: "I believe in Jesús."

"You, ma'am, are not my daughter," murmurs Martín now, like a mantra. That night he writes to Bruno saying: All's well.

One afternoon, on the way back from the supermarket, he finds that someone has put up posters on top of his. He goes up and down the street and confirms that right where he'd posted his flyers, there are now signs announcing the disappearance of a husky-shepherd mix named Pancho. There is a decent reward of twenty thousand pesos. Martín jots down the number and the name Paz, Pancho's owner.

There is a bottle of Jack Daniel's in the kitchen. Martín only drinks beer or wine, he's not used to liquor, but on a whim he pours a glass, and with each sip, he discovers that he likes Jack Daniel's, that he loves it. So by the time he decides to call Paz, he's fairly drunk. "You put your dog over my cat," is the first thing he says to her, awkwardly, vehemently.

It's ten thirty at night. Paz seems surprised but says she understands the situation. He regrets his heated tone, and the conversation ends in listless mutual apologies. Before hanging up, Martín catches a voice in the background, a complaint. A child's voice.

The following morning Martín watches through the window as a young woman on a bicycle tackles the time-consuming task of moving the posters. He goes out to the street and looks at her from a certain distance—she isn't beautiful, he thinks, making up his mind, she's just young, she must be around twenty years old, Martín could be her father (although he doesn't think this last part). Paz pulls down her posters and finds space for them above or below his. She disguises the torn corners by folding them, and while she's at it, she adjusts Martín's posters, too. She works skillfully, and he wonders if she does this for a living: just as there are people who work as dog walkers, she must be part of a squad of lost-animal seekers, Martín thinks. This is not the case.

He introduces himself and apologizes again for having called so late the night before. He accompanies her the rest of the way down the street. At first she seems reticent, but then the conversation begins to take shape. They talk about Mississippi and about Pancho and also about pets in general, about the responsibility of owning pets, and even about the word *pet*, which she doesn't like because she finds it derogatory. Martín smokes several cigarettes while they talk, but he doesn't want to toss the butts. He holds them in his hand as if they were valuable. "There's a trash can over there," Paz says suddenly, and the sentence coincides with the corner where they have to part ways.

That night he calls her and tells her that he's covered dozens of blocks looking for Mississippi, and he's also kept an eye out for Pancho. It sounds like a lie, but it's true. She thanks him for the gesture, but doesn't let the conversation flow from there. Martín begins to call her daily, and though the conversations stay short, he feels good about them, as if those few sentences are enough to establish some kind of presence.

A week later he sees a dog that looks like Pancho close to the house. He tries to approach it, but the dog runs away scared. He calls Paz, but he has trouble talking. What he has to say sounds like a lie again, like an excuse to see her. But

Paz accepts it. They meet and patrol side streets for a while, until it's time for her to go pick her son up from kindergarten. Martín insists on going with her.

"I can't believe you have a son," he says.

"Sometimes I can't believe it, either," replies Paz.

"Another boyfriend," is the first thing the child says when he sees Martín. He drags his little backpack expressively behind him without looking Martín in the face, but Paz tells him Martín thinks he's seen Pancho and this gets the boy's hopes up; he insists they keep looking for the dog. They cover many blocks, and they could easily pass for a perfect family. They say goodbye when they reach Paz's house. Both of them know that they will see each other again, and maybe the boy knows it, too.

It's been over a month since Mississippi's disappearance, and Martín doesn't hold out any hope of finding him. He even composes a confused and apologetic email to Bruno, but he doesn't dare send it. The cat returns, however, one morning at dawn, barely able to push through his door; he's covered in wounds and has an enormous ball of pus on his back. The vet is pessimistic but does an emergency operation and prescribes some antibiotics that Martín has to give Mississippi daily. He has to feed the cat baby food and clean his wounds every eight hours. The poor cat is so battered and weak that he can't move or meow.

Martín focuses on Mississippi's health. Now he loves the cat, takes care of him for real. He forgets to call Paz for a few days. She is finally the one to call him one morning, and she's happy to hear the good news. Half an hour later they are sitting beside the cat, petting him, pitying him.

"You told me you lived alone, but this seems like a family's house," she declares suddenly, looking at the photo of Consuelo. Martín gets nervous and delays his answer. Finally he tells her, downcast and murmuring, as if it were painful to remember: "We've been separated for several months, maybe a year. My wife and our daughter went to live in an apartment, and I stayed here with the cat."

"Your wife is beautiful," says Paz, looking at the photo on the wall.

"But she's not my wife anymore," answers Martín.

"But she's beautiful," repeats Paz. "And you never told me you had a daughter."

"We just met, we can't say words like 'never' and 'always' yet," says Martín. "And I don't like to talk about her," he adds. "It makes me sad. I'm still not over the breakup. The worst part is that Consuelo doesn't let me see my daughter, she wants more money," he says. Paz looks at him anxiously, her mouth half open. He should be feeling the adrenaline that emboldens the liar, but he gets distracted looking at those small, slightly separated teeth, the aquiline nose, those thin but well-formed legs that seem perfect to him.

"You had your daughter very young," Paz says to him.

"Not really," he replies, "Or maybe so. Maybe I was too young." Now he is completely tangled up in the lie.

"I got pregnant at sixteen, and I almost had an abortion," says Paz, maybe to balance out Martín's confessions.

"Why didn't you?" Martín asks. It's a stupid, offensive question, but she's unfazed.

"Because abortion is illegal in Chile," she says very seriously, but then she laughs, and her eyes shine. "That year," she goes on, "my two best friends got pregnant: I was going to get an abortion at the same place they did, but at the last minute, I changed my mind and decided to have the baby."

They have sex on the sofa, and at first it seems like a good lay, but he comes too soon and apologizes.

"Don't worry," she replies. "You're better than most boys my age." Martín thinks about that word, 'boys,' which he would never use, but which sounds so appropriate, so natural, coming from her. She has almost no freckles on her face or arms, but her body is covered in them. Her back looks like it was spattered with red ink. He likes it.

They start seeing each other daily, and they keep looking for Pancho. The possibility of finding him is by now remote, but Paz doesn't lose hope. Then they go back to the house and tend to Mississippi together. The wounds are healing slowly but well, and on his back, where the doctor shaved his fur, they can already see a finer, lighter fur growing in. The romance also progresses, and at an accelerated speed. Sometimes he likes this acceleration, he needs it. But he also wants it all to end: to be forced to tell the truth, for it all to go to shit. One day, Paz notices that Martín has taken the photo of Consuelo down. She asks him to hang it up again. He asks her why.

"I don't want us to get confused," she says. He doesn't really understand, but he hangs the photo again. "If it bothers you to have sex in the bed where you slept and had sex with your wife," Paz tells him, "I'd understand." He shakes his head emphatically and tells her that for some time now—that's the expression he uses, "for some time now"—he hasn't thought about his wife.

"Really, sorry to insist," she says, "but if it bothers you to fuck here, you have to tell me."

"We almost never had sex anymore, anyway," replies Martín, and they are silent until she asks him if he had ever had sex with his wife on the table in the living room. He gives her a horny smile and says that he had not. The game continues, vertiginous and fun. She asks if his wife had ever dipped his dick in condensed milk before sucking it, or if perhaps, by chance, his wife had liked him to stick three fingers in her ass, or if there'd been a time when she'd asked him to come on her face, on her tits, on her ass, in her hair.

One of those mornings, Paz shows up with a rosebush and a bougainvillea. He gets a shovel, and together they construct a minimal garden in the empty plot by the entrance. He digs clumsily, so Paz takes the shovel away from him, and in a matter of minutes, the job is done.

"Sorry," Martín tells her. "I know the guy is supposed to do the hard part."

"No worries," she answers, and adds cheerfully: "I was born under democracy." Later, apropos of nothing, maybe as a way of anticipating his eventual confession, Martín launches into a monologue about the past, in which brushstrokes of the truth are mixed with some obligatory lies, as he searches for a way of being honest, or at least less dishonest. He talks about pain, about the difficulty of building simple, long-lasting ties with other people. "I'm addicted to the drug of solitude," is his crowning statement. She listens attentively, compassionately, and nods her head several times in affirmation, but after a pause in which she adjusts her hair, settles into the armchair, and kicks off her sneakers, she says it again, mischievously: "I was born under democracy." And at lunch, when she sees him cutting his chicken off the bone with a knife and fork, she says she'd rather eat with her hands because she was "born under democracy." The phrase works for everything, especially in bed: when he wants to do it without a condom, when he asks her to not make so much noise or to be careful about walking around the living room naked, and when she moves so savagely and eagerly on top that Martín can't hide the pain in his penis—to all of these things, she responds that she was born under democracy, or else she simply says, shrugging her shoulders: "Democracy!"

Time goes by with happy indolence. There are hours, maybe entire days when Martín manages to forget who he really is. He forgets he is pretending, that he's lying, that he's guilty. On two occasions, however, he almost comes out with the truth. But the truth is long. Telling the truth would require many words. And there are only two weeks left. No! One week.

Now he's driving, nervous: it's Friday, and tomorrow he has to go to a wedding as Paz's date. She asked him if they could take the car, so now he only has one day to practice—he has to seem like a seasoned driver, or at least he has to obey the traffic laws. At first it all goes well. He stalls at a red light, as he tends to do, but he has some courage left, and for a little while he achieves a certain fluidity. Then he gets carried away and decides to go to the mall to buy two plates and three cups to replace the ones that he's broken, but he's unable to change lanes at the right time, or move ahead of the other cars, and he gets stuck in his lane for ten minutes, until the exits run out. Now he's headed southward on the highway, and there's nothing to do but attempt a dangerous U-turn.

He pulls over onto the median and decides to wait until he calms down. He turns off the radio and bides time until he can pull the U-turn, but, when the opening comes, the car stalls again, and he's left at the mercy of an oncoming truck. The driver swerves to avoid him and leans on the horn.

He backs up and returns to the southbound highway, and every once in a while he thinks about attempting another U-turn or trying to get off the highway, but he's paralyzed with fear and all he can do is keep going in this straight line. He comes to a tollbooth and slams on the brakes; the toll collector smiles at him, but he's incapable of smiling back. He can only keep going, like a slow automaton, until he reaches Rancagua.

I've never been to Rancagua, he thinks, ashamed. He gets out of the car, looks at the people, tries to guess the time from the movement in the Plaza de Armas: twelve—no, eleven. It's early, but he's hungry, so he buys an empanada. He stays there a full hour, parked, smoking, thinking about Paz. Such weighty names annoy him—they're so full, so directly symbolic: Paz, Consuelo—peace and consolation. He thinks that, if he ever has a child, he's going to make up a name that doesn't mean anything. Then he takes twenty-four turns around the plaza—though he doesn't count them—and some teenage girls playing hooky eye him strangely. He parks again and his phone rings; he tells Paz he's at the supermarket. She wants to see him. He replies that he can't because he has to pick his daughter up from school.

"Finally, you can see her?" she asks, jubilant.

"Yes. We came to an agreement," he says.

"I'd love to meet her," says Paz.

"Not yet," replies Martín. "Down the road."

Not until four in the afternoon does he start heading back. The trip is painless this time, or less tense. I've just learned to really drive, he thinks that night before going to sleep, a little bit proud.

And yet, on Saturday, on the way to the wedding, he stalls the car. He says his eyes feel "caustic"—he's not sure that's the right word, but he uses it. Paz takes the wheel—she doesn't have a license but it doesn't matter. He watches her drive, concentrated on the road, the seat belt between her breasts. He feels an anticipatory pain, the foreboding of his future loss. He drinks a lot at the wedding. A lot. And even so, everything is good. He makes a good impression, he's a good dancer, he cracks some good jokes. Paz's friends congratulate her. She takes off her red shoes and dances barefoot, and he thinks it's absurd that he questioned her beauty at first: she's beautiful, she's free, she's fun, she is marvelous. He feels the desire to tell her right there, in the middle of the dance floor, that all is lost, irreversibly lost. That the family is returning on Wednesday. He goes back to the table, watches her dance with her girlfriends, with the groom, with the groom's father. Martín orders another Jack Daniel's and drinks it in one gulp. He likes the grating pain in his throat. He looks at the chair where Paz's purse and shoes are: he thinks about keeping those red shoes, like a caricature of a fetishist.

The next day is a hungover one. He wakes up at eleven thirty and there's a strange song playing, a kind of new age music that Paz hums along with while she cooks. She'd gotten up early, gone out to buy fish and a ton of vegetables, which she's now frying in the wok, slowly stirring in the soy sauce. After lunch, stretched out naked on the bed, Martín counts the freckles on her back, on her ass, on Paz's legs: 223. It's the moment to confess everything, and he even thinks that she'll understand: she'll get mad, she'll mock him, she'll refuse to see him for weeks, for months, she'll be confused and all of that, but she will forgive him. He starts to talk, timidly, searching for the right tone, but she cuts him off and leaves to go pick up her son, who is at her parents' house.

They come back at five. Up to this point the boy had been reticent with Martín, but this time he loosens up and is more trusting. For the first time ever, they play together. First they try to cheer up Mississippi, who is still convalescing, but soon they give up. Then the boy puts the tomatoes next to the oranges and tells Martín he wants some orange juice. Martín picks up the tomatoes, and when he's about to cut the first one the boy cries, "Noooooo!" They repeat the routine twelve, fifteen times. There is a variation: before cutting the tomato, Martín catches on and feigns fury, saying that the grocer sold him tomatoes instead of oranges, pretending that he's going to storm back and complain, all so the boy will say, intoxicated with joy, "Nooooooo!"

Now they're playing with the remote control. The boy pushes a button and Martín falls down, bites his own hand, shouts, or goes mute.

What if I really did lose my voice? he thinks later, while the child sleeps on his mother's lap.

If only they'd turn my volume down, thinks Martín.

If only they'd fast-forward me, rewind me. If only they'd record over me.

If only they'd erase me.

Now Paz, her son, and Mississippi are asleep, and Martín has been locked in the study for hours doing who knows what, maybe crying.

They like what they see at first, when they get out of the taxi. Consuelo looks at the bougainvillea and the rosebush, and she wants to find Martín right away to thank him for that gesture. Then they are surprised to see the photo of Consuelo on the main wall, and in the confusion she even thinks, for a split second, that the photo has always been there, but no, of course it hasn't. They go through the house, alarmed, and their confusion grows as they look into each of the bedrooms—it's clear that Martín moved the boxes and wardrobes around, and every minute brings a new discovery: stains on the curtains, cigarette ash on the carpet. The cat is in Sofi's room, sleeping on top of the stuffed animals.

They look over his wounds, which still haven't scarred over completely, and they are furious at first, but then grateful, after all, that he's alive. In the kitchen they find some used syringes, along with the medicine and prescriptions.

Martín isn't there and he doesn't answer his cell phone. There is no note to even attempt to explain the situation. They can't understand what has happened. It's difficult to understand. At first they think Martín robbed them and Bruno anxiously looks over the bookshelves, but he finds no evidence of theft.

He feels stupid for having trusted Martín. They had exchanged so many emails, and there'd been no reason to suspect anything. "These things happen," says Consuelo, for her part, but she says it automatically, without conviction. Every so often Bruno calls Martín again, leaving messages on his voice mail that are sometimes friendly and other times violent.

A few days later, the doorbell rings very early in the morning. Consuelo goes out to answer. "Can I help you?" she asks a young woman, who is frozen, recognizing her. "What do you want?" Consuelo asks. She takes a while to answer. She stares again, intently, at Consuelo, and with a gesture of contempt, or of supreme sadness, she answers: "Nothing."

"Who was it?" asks Bruno from the bedroom. Consuelo closes the door and hesitates a second before answering: "No one."

Artist's Rendition

Yasna fired the gun into her father's chest and then suffocated him with a pillow. He was a gym teacher, and she wasn't anything, she was no one.

But she is now: now she is someone who has killed, someone who sits in jail waiting for her shitty food and remembering her father's blood, dark and thick. She doesn't write about that, though. She only writes love letters.

Only love letters, as if that weren't enough.

But it isn't true that she killed her father. That murder never happened. Nor does she write love letters, she never has, maybe because she knows almost nothing about love, and what she does know, she doesn't like. What she does know is monstrous. The one doing the writing is someone else, someone urgently recalling her, not because he misses her or wants to see her, but simply because he was commissioned, a few months ago now, to write a detective story. Preferably one set in Chile. And right away he thought of her, of Yasna, of that crime that was never committed, and although he had dozens of other stories to choose from, some of them more docile, easier to turn into detective stories, he thought that Yasna's story deserved to be told, or at least that he would be able to tell it.

He took a few notes at the time, but then he had to focus on other obligations. Now he has only one day left to write it.

The innocent part of the story, the least useful part, the part he won't include and that he doesn't even fully remember—since his job consists, also, of forgetting, or rather of pretending that he remembers what he has forgotten—begins in the summertime, toward the end of the eighties, when both of them were fourteen years old. He wasn't even interested in literature yet; back then, the only thing that held his interest was chasing certain women, with timidity but also persistence. But it's an overstatement to call them women—they weren't women yet, just as he was not yet a man. Although Yasna was several times more a woman than he was a man.

Yasna lived a few blocks away. She spent her afternoons in the messy front yard of her house, surrounded by roses, rue plants, and foxtails, sitting on a stool with a pad of drawing paper on her lap. "What are you drawing?" he asked her one afternoon from the other side of the fence, momentarily emboldened, and she smiled, not because she wanted to smile, but reflexively. In reply she held up the pad, and from a distance it seemed to him that there was a face sketched on the paper. He didn't know if it was a man's or a woman's, but he thought he could tell it was a face.

They didn't become friends, but they went on talking every once in a while. Two months later she invited him to her birthday party, and he, oozing happiness, going for broke, bought her a globe in the bookstore on the plaza. He left for the party on time, but on the way there he ran into Danilo, who was smoking a joint with another friend on the corner—they had a ton of weed, they'd started growing it a while ago, but still hadn't made up their minds to sell it. Danilo offered him the joint, and he took four or five deep drags, and straight-away he felt the dulling effect that he knew well, though he didn't smoke with any real frequency. "What've you got there?" Danilo asked, and he'd been waiting for that question, hiding the bag precisely to elicit it: "The world," he replied with glee. They carefully removed the cellophane wrapping and spent some time searching for countries. Danilo wanted to find Sweden, but couldn't. "Look how big that country is," he said, pointing to the Soviet Union. They finished the joint before parting ways.

Yasna seemed to be the only one taking the party seriously. She wore a blue dress down to her knees, her eyes were lined and her eyelashes curled and darkened, and there was a bashful sky blue on her eyelids. The cassette tape that played in its entirety was no longer in fashion, or it was in fashion only among the more or less fifteen guests crammed into the living room. It was clear they were all good friends, because they changed partners in the middle of the songs, which they sang along to enthusiastically, though they knew absolutely no English.

He felt out of place, but Yasna looked over at him every two minutes, every five minutes, and the rhythm of those glances competed with the lethargy from the weed. After gulping two tall glasses of Kem Piña, he sat down at the dining room table as a new cassette started to play, Duran Duran this time, also in its entirety. No-no-notorious. They danced to it strangely, as if it were a polka, or one of those old ballroom dances. It all seemed ridiculous to him, but he wouldn't have said no to joining in, he would have danced well, he thought suddenly, with an inexplicable touch of resentment, and then he turned his attention to the chips, to the shoe-string potatoes, the cheese cut into uneven cubes, the nuts, and a few dozen multicolored popcorn balls that struck him, who knows why, as interesting.

He doesn't remember the details, except for the sudden lash of hunger, the wound of hunger: the munchies. He made an effort to eat at a normal speed, but when Yasna came in with tortilla chips and an immense bowl of guacamole, he lost all control. Tortilla chips and guacamole had only recently been introduced in Chile, he had never tried them before and he didn't even know that was what they were called, but after trying one he couldn't stop, even though he knew everyone was watching him; it seemed like they were taking turns looking at him. He had bits of avocado and tomato on his fingers, and grease from the chips; his mouth hurt, he felt half-chewed bits of food stuck in his molars, which he extricated tenaciously with his tongue. He ate the entire bowl almost by himself, it was scandalous. And still he wanted to go on eating.

Just then the door to the kitchen opened and a white light hit him right in the face. A man came out; he was fairly fat but brawny, his parted hair divided into two identical halves combed back with gel. It was Yasna's father. Beside him was a younger man, very similar in appearance, you might say good-looking if it weren't for the scar from a cleft lip, though perhaps that imperfection made him more attractive. And here ends, perhaps, the innocent part of the story: when they grab him tightly by the arm and he tries desperately to go on eating, and a few moments later, after a long and confused series of hard looks and clipped sentences, of scraping and dragging, when he feels a kick in his right thigh followed by dozens of kicks on his ass, his shins, his back. He's on the floor, enduring the pain, with Yasna's sobbing and some unintelligible shouts in the background; he wants to defend himself, but he barely manages to shield his groin. It's the second man who is beating him, the one Yasna will later call "the assistant." Yasna's father stands there and watches, laughing the way bad guys laugh in lousy movies and sometimes also in real life.

Although none of this, in essence, is relevant to his story, he tries to remember if it was cold that night (no), if there was a moon (waning), if it was Friday or Saturday (it was Saturday), if anyone tried, in all the confusion, to defend him (no). He puts his clothes on over his pajamas, because it's the middle of winter and much too cold to change, and as he drives to the service station to buy kerosene, he thinks with confidence, with optimism, that he has all morning to work on his notes and in the afternoon he will write nonstop, for four or five hours, and then he'll even have enough time, in the evening, to go with a friend to try out the new Peruvian restaurant that opened up near his house. He fills the gas cans, and now he's at the Esso market, drinking coffee, chewing on a ham-and-cheese sandwich, and thumbing through the newspaper that came free with the coffee and ham-and-cheese sandwich. What they want from him is simply a blood-soaked Latin American story, he thinks, and in the margins of the news he jots down a series of decisions that take shape harmoniously, naturally, like the promise of a peaceful day at work: the father will be named Feliciano, and she will be

Joana; the assistant and Danilo are no good, nor is the marijuana, maybe a hard drug instead, and though he doesn't really want to make Feliciano into a drug trafficker—too hackneyed—he does think it's necessary to move the protagonists down in class, because the middle class—and he thinks this without irony—is a problem if one wants to write Latin American literature. He needs a Santiago slum where it's not unusual to see teenagers in the plazas cracked out or huffing paint thinner.

Nor will it work for Feliciano to be a gym teacher. He imagines him unemployed instead, humiliated and jobless at the start of the eighties, or later, surviving in the work programs of the dictatorship, endlessly sweeping the same bit of sidewalk, or maybe as a snitch who informs on suspicious activity in the neighborhood, or maybe even knifing someone to the ground. Or maybe as a cop, one who comes home late and shouts for his food, and who has no qualms about threatening his daughter at night with the same billy club he used to beat back protesters at noon.

He has some doubts at this point, but they're nothing serious.

Nothing is that serious, he thinks: it's just a ten-page text, fifteen pages tops, he doesn't have to waste time on the backstory. Two or three resonant phrases, a few well-placed adjectives will fix any problems. He parks, takes the gas cans out of the trunk, and then, while he fills the heater's tank, he imagines Joana splashing kerosene all over the house with her father inside—too sensationalist, he thinks. He prefers a gun, maybe because he remembers that there *was* a gun in Yasna's house, that when she said she was going to kill her father she mentioned the gun in the house.

There was a gun, of course there was, but it was only an air rifle, which had lain idle for years in the closet, a vestige of the time when her father used to go to the country with his friends to hunt partridge and rabbit. Only once, one spring Sunday, coming back from church when she was seven years old, did Yasna see him fire it. He was in the yard, downing a beer and taking aim with a steady hand at the kites in the sky over the park. He hit the bull's-eye four times: the owners couldn't understand what was happening. Yasna thought about those parents and children from other neighborhoods watching disconcertedly as their kites foundered and crashed, but she didn't say anything. Later she asked him if you could kill someone with that rifle, and he replied that no, it was only used for hunting. "Though if you got the guy in the head from close up," her father clarified after a while, "you'd fuck him up pretty good."

After the party, the writer—who at that time didn't even dream of becoming a writer, though he dreamed about many other things, almost all of them better than being a writer— was terribly scared and didn't make any effort to see Yasna again. He avoided the street that led to her house, all the streets that led to her house, and he didn't go to church, either, since he knew that she went to church, though in any case that didn't take a lot of effort, because by then he had stopped believing in God.

Six years passed before their paths crossed again. He saw her by chance, in the city center. Yasna's hair was straighter and longer, and she was wearing the uniform they'd given her at work. He was wearing a plaid flannel shirt and combat boots, his hair disheveled, as if he wanted to exemplify the

fashion of the times—or the part of fashion that corresponded to him, a literature student. By then he could be
called a writer, he had written some stories. Whether they
were good or bad was not important—a writer is someone
who writes, a little or a lot, but who writes, just as a murderer
is someone who kills, whether they've claimed one person or
many, whether their victims are strangers or their fathers.
And it isn't fair to say that she was nothing, then, that she
was no one, because she was a cashier at a bank. She didn't
like the work, but she also didn't think—nor does she think
now—that there was such a thing as a job she would like.

While they drank Nescafé at a diner they talked about the
beating, and she tried to explain what had happened, though
she said she wasn't very clear on that herself. Then she talked
about her childhood, especially about her mother's death in a
car crash, how she'd barely gotten to know her, and she also
talked about the assistant, which was how her father had first
introduced the man to her while they were varnishing some
wicker chairs in the yard, although some days later he told
her, as if it weren't important, that actually the assistant was
the son of a friend who had died, that he didn't have anywhere to go and so he'd be living with them for a while. The
assistant was twenty-four years old then; he came home late
at night, slept most of the morning, didn't work or study, but
sometimes he babysat Yasna, mostly on Tuesdays, when her
father got home at midnight after practicing with his basketball team, and Saturdays, when her father had games and
then went out with his teammates to drink a few beers. The
writer didn't understand why she was telling him all this, as
if he didn't know (and maybe he didn't, although, by that
point, since he was already a writer, he *should* have known)

that this was the way people get to know each other, by telling each other irrelevant things, by airing their words blithely, irresponsibly, until they reach dangerous territories, places where words need the varnish of silence.

Although the conversation wasn't over, he asked if she had a phone, if they could see each other again, because right now he had to leave for a party. She shrugged, and maybe she was waiting for him to invite her to that party, though she couldn't go anyway, but he didn't, and then she didn't want to give him her number, and she also forbade him from showing up at her house, even though the assistant no longer lived there.

"Then how will we see each other?" he asked again, and she, again, shrugged her shoulders.

But she'd mentioned the name of the bank where she worked, which had only three branches, so he was able to track her down a few weeks later, and they began a routine of lunches, almost always at a fried-chicken place on Calle Bandera, other times at a greasy spoon on Teatinos, and occasionally, when one of them had more money, at Naturista. He went on hoping for something more to happen, but she was elusive and talked about a boyfriend who was so generous and understanding he seemed obviously fabricated. Sometimes, for long stretches, he watched her talk but didn't listen to her. He looked most of all at her mouth, her teeth, perfect except for the stains from cigarette smoke on the front ones. He would do this until she raised or lowered her voice, or maybe let slip some unexpected bit of information, as she did one time with a sentence that, although he hadn't the slightest idea what she'd been talking about, brought him back to the present, though she didn't say it in the tone of a confession: on the contrary, she pronounced it without dramatics, almost like a joke, as if it were possible for a sentence like that to be a joke. "I didn't have a happy childhood" was what she said, and he didn't understand what he should have understood, what anyone today would understand, but hearing her say that still shook him, or at least woke him up.

Did she really use that word, so formal, so literary: *childhood*? Maybe she said "when I was a kid," or "when I was little." In any case, in the past, ten or fifteen years ago, say, and definitely thirty, it would have been necessary to tell the entire story, cultivating a sense of mystery, laboring over the dramatic effects, procuring a gradual and eventually shocking emotion. Good writers and also bad ones knew how to do this, and it didn't seem immoral to them, they even enjoyed it, to the extent that depicting a story always brings a certain kind of pleasure. But what good would that mystery do now, what kind of pleasure could be gained when the sentence that says it all has already been let out into the world? Because there are some phrases that have won their freedom: sentences we have learned how to hear, to read, to write. Fifteen, thirty years back, good writers, and bad ones, too, would have trusted in a sentence like that to introduce a mystery that they would explain only at the end, with a scene of the father asleep and the assistant in the bedroom touching the nipples of a ten-year-old girl, who is surprised but, as if it were a game of Monkey See, Monkey Do, puts her own hand under the assistant's shirt and, with utter innocence, touches his nipple in return.

Another scene, two days later. The father is at basketball practice, and the assistant calls her into his room, closes the door, takes off her clothes, and leaves her locked in. The girl doesn't resist, she stays there, she searches among his clothes, which are still in bags as if, though he's lived there for months now, he had just arrived or were about to leave—the girl tries on shirts and some enormous blue jeans, and she's dying to look at herself in the mirror, but there's no mirror in the assistant's room, so she turns on a little black-and-white TV on the nightstand, and there's a drama on that isn't the one she watches, but the knob spins all the way around, and she ends up getting sucked into the plot anyway, and that's what she's doing when she hears voices in the living room. The assistant appears with two other guys, and he takes the clothes she's found off her, threatens her with the bottle of Escudo beer he holds in his left hand, she cries and the guys all laugh, drunk, sitting on the floor. One of them says, "But she doesn't have any tits or pubes, man," and the other replies, "But she's got two holes."

The assistant doesn't let them touch her, though. "She's all mine," he says, and throws them out. Then he puts on some grotesque music, Pachuco, maybe, and orders her to dance. She's crying on the floor like she would during a tantrum. "I'm sorry," he consoles her later, while he runs his hand over the girl's naked back, her still shapeless ass, her white toothpick legs. That day in his room he puts two fingers inside her and pauses, he caresses her and insults her with words she has never heard before. Then he begins, with the brutal efficiency of a pedagogue, to show her the correct way to suck it, and when she makes a dangerous, involuntary movement, he warns her that if she bites it he will kill her. "Next time you're gonna have to swallow," he tells her afterward, with that high voice some Chilean men have when they're trying to sound indulgent.

He never ejaculated inside her, he preferred to finish on her face, and later, when Yasna's body took shape, on her breasts, on her ass. It wasn't clear that he liked these changes; over the five years that he raped her, he lost interest, or desire, several times. Yasna was grateful for these reprieves, but her feelings were ambiguous, muddled, maybe because in some way she thought she belonged to the assistant, who by that point didn't even bother to make her promise not to tell anyone. The father would come home from work, fix himself some tea, greet his daughter and the assistant, then ask them if they needed anything. He'd hand a thousand pesos to him and five hundred to her, and then he'd shut himself in for hours to watch the TV dramas, the news, the variety show, the news again, and the sitcom *Cheers*, which he loved, at the end of the lineup. Sometimes he heard noises, and when the noises got too loud he connected some headphones to the TV.

It was in fact the assistant who urged Yasna to organize her fifteenth-birthday party ("You deserve it, you're a good, normal girl," he told her). At that point he'd been uninterested for several months; he would touch her only every once in a while. That night, however, after beating up the writer, when it was almost dawn, the assistant, drunk and a little jealous, informed Yasna in the unequivocal tone of an order that from then on they would sleep in the same room, that now they would be like man and wife, and only then did the father, who was also completely drunk, tell him that was impossible, he couldn't go on fucking his sister—the assistant defended himself by saying she was only his half sister—and that was how she found out they were related. Completely out of control, his eyes full of hatred, the assistant started to hit Yasna's father, who he had always known was also his father, and he even gave Yasna a punch on the side of her head before he left.

He said he was leaving for good and in the end he kept his word. But during the months that followed she was afraid he would come back, and sometimes she also wanted him to. One night when she felt scared she went to sleep with her clothes on, next to her father. Two nights. The third night they slept in an embrace, and also on the fourth, the fifth. On night number six, at dawn, she felt her father's thumb palpating her ass. Maybe she shed a tear before she felt her father's fat penis inside her, but she didn't cry any more than that, because by then she didn't cry anymore, just as she no longer smiled when she wanted to smile: the equivalent of a smile, what she did when she felt the desire to smile, she carried out in a different way, with a different part of her body, or only in her head, in her imagination. Sex was for her still the only thing it had ever been: something arduous, rough, but above all mechanical.

The writer has a simple lunch of cream of asparagus soup with half a glass of wine. Then he sprawls in an armchair next to the stove with a blanket over himself. He sleeps only ten minutes, which is still more than enough time for an eventful dream, one with many possibilities and impossibilities that he forgets as soon as he wakes up, but he retains this scene: he's driving down the same highway as always, toward San Antonio, in a car that has the driver's seat on the right, and everything seems under control, but as he approaches the tollbooth he's invaded by anxiety about explaining his situation to the toll collector. He's afraid the woman will die of fright when she sees the empty seat where the driver should be. The volume of that thought rises until it becomes deafening: when she sees that nobody is driving the car, the toll collector—in the dream it's one woman in particular, one he always remembers for the way she has of tying back her hair, and for her strange nose, long and crooked but not necessarily ugly—will die of fright. "I'm going to get out quickly," he thinks in the dream. "I'll explain." He decides to stop the car a few meters before he reaches the booth and get out with his hands up, like someone who wants to show he isn't armed, but the moment never takes place, because although the booth is close, the car takes an infinite amount of time to reach it.

He writes the dream down, but he falsifies it, fleshes it out—he always does that, he can't help but embellish his dreams when he transcribes them, decorating them with false scenes, with words that are more lifelike or completely fantastic and that insinuate departures, conclusions, surprising twists. As he writes it, the toll collector is Yasna, and it's true that in an indirect, subterranean way, they are similar. Suddenly he understands the discovery here, the shift: instead of working at a bank, Joana will be a tollbooth collector, which is one of the worst possible jobs. He pictures her reaching out her hand, trying to grab all the coins, loving and hating the drivers or maybe completely indifferent to them. He imagines the smell of the coins on her hands. He imagines her with her shoes off and legs spread apart—the only license she can take in that cell—and later on a bus, on her way home, dozing off and planning the murder, now fully convinced that it is, as they say in mass, truly right and just. After she's committed the crime she heads south, sleeps in a hostel in Puerto Montt, and gets as far as Dalcahue or Quemchi, where she hopes to find a job and forget everything, but she makes some absurd, desperate mistakes.

The last time he saw Yasna, they almost had sex. Up until then they'd seen each other only during those lunches in the city center; whenever he'd asked her to go to the movies or out dancing, she'd pile on the excuses and talk vaguely about her perfect, made-up boyfriend. But one day she called the writer and then showed up at his house. They watched a movie and then they were going to go to the plaza, but halfway there she changed her mind and they ended up at Danilo's, smoking weed and drinking burgundy. The three of them were there, in the living room, high as kites and lying on the rug, carefree and happy, when Danilo tried to kiss her and she affectionately pushed him away. Later, half an hour, maybe an hour later, she told them that in another world, in a perfect world, she would sleep with both of them, and with whoever else she wanted, but that in this shitty world she couldn't sleep with anyone. There was weight in her words, an eloquence that should have fascinated them, and maybe it did, maybe they were fascinated, but really they just looked lost.

After a while Danilo let out a laugh, or a sneeze. "If you want a perfect world, smoke another one," he told her, and he went to his room to watch TV. Yasna and the writer stayed in the living room, and even though there was no music, Yasna started to dance, and without much preamble she took off her dress and bra. Astonished as he was, he kissed her awkwardly, he touched her breasts, caressed her between her legs, he took off her underwear and slowly licked the down on her pubis, which wasn't black like her hair, but brown. Then she got dressed again suddenly and apologized, she told him she couldn't, that she was sorry, but it wasn't possible. "Why not?" he asked, and in his question there was confusion, but there was also love—he doesn't remember it, he would be incapable of remembering it, but there was love.

"Because we're friends," she said.

"We're not such great friends," he answered, completely serious, and he repeated it many times. Yasna let out a peal of beautiful, stoned laughter, a real and delicious guffaw that only very gradually wore itself out, that lasted ten minutes, fifteen minutes, until finally she managed to find her way, with difficulty, back to a serious and resonant tone with which it would be appropriate to tell him that this was a goodbye, that they could never see each other again. He didn't understand, but he knew there was no sense in asking questions. They sat in a corner with their arms around each other. He took Yasna's right hand and calmly began to gnaw at her fingernails. He doesn't remember this, but while he looked at her and bit her nails he was thinking that he didn't know her, that he would never know her.

Before they left they sat for a while with Danilo in front of the TV, watching an eternal game of tennis. She drank four cups of tea at an impressive speed, and she ate two marraqueta rolls. "Where's your mom?" she asked Danilo suddenly.

"Over at an aunt's house," he said.

"And where's your dad?"

"I don't have a dad," he replied. And then she said:

"You're lucky. I do have one, but I'm going to kill him. In my house there's a rifle, and I'm going to kill my father. And I'll go to jail and I'll be happy."

By now it's three in the afternoon, he doesn't have much time left. He urgently turns on the computer, annoyed by the seconds the system takes to start up. He writes the first five pages in a matter of minutes, from the moment the detective arrives at the scene of the crime and realizes he has been there before, that it's Joana's house, until he climbs up to the attic and finds the old boxes with clothes from the time when they were a couple, because in the story they were a couple, but not for very long, and in secret. He also finds the globe he'd given her—but without the stand that held it—and a backpack he thinks he recognizes in among the fishing rods and reels, the buckets and shovels for the beach, the sleeping bags and rusted dumbbells. He keeps looking around, impelled more by nostalgia than a desire to find evidence, and then, just like in books, in movies, and also sometimes in reality, he finds something that would not be conclusive to anyone else, but that is, immediately, to him: a box full of drawings, hundreds of drawings, all portraits of her father, ordered by date or series, each more realistic than the last, at first sketched in pencil, and then, the majority, in the green ink of a Bic fine-point pen. When he sees the accentuated contours, gone over so many times that the paper is often torn, and the exaggerated features—though never to the point of caricature, they never lose the aura of realism—the detective understands what he should have understood a long time before, what he hadn't known how to read, what he hadn't known how to say, how to do.

The writer works at a cruising speed through the intermediate scenes and takes great pains over the final two pages, when the detective finds Joana in a boardinghouse in Dalcahue and promises to protect her. She tells him in great detail about the murder, put off so many times over the course of her life, and while she cries she seems to grow calmer. Maybe they stay together, after all, but it's not certain. The ending is delicate, elegantly ambiguous, though it's not clear what it is the writer thinks is ambiguous, or delicate, or elegant about it.

It's not a great story, but he sends it off with a clear conscience, and he even has time to drink a pisco sour and eat some yuca a la huancaína before his friends get to the Peruvian restaurant.

It's not a great story, no. But Yasna would like it.

Yasna would like the story, though she doesn't read, she doesn't like to read. But if it were made into a movie, she would watch it to the end. And if she caught a rerun of it and didn't remember it, or even if she remembered it well, she would watch it again. She doesn't often watch movies, in truth, nor does she often recall the writer. She doesn't even know he is a writer. She did remember him a few months ago, though, when she was walking in the neighborhood where he used to live.

The doctors had declared her father terminally ill and recommended she give him marijuana to help with the pain. She'd thought of Danilo's plants, hence that walk through the old neighborhood, which seemed erratic but was not: she enjoyed the luxury of walking around aimlessly, peripherally, reaching the end of a street, even, and then retracing her steps as if searching for an address. But she knew perfectly well where Danilo lived, still in his family home; she merely wanted to enjoy that luxury, modest as it was. Her father was sleeping calmly—he was having a good day, with less pain than last week—so she could go out for a walk and take her time.

"I hope you haven't killed your dad," Danilo said when he finally recognized her, and since she didn't remember her words from that night almost twenty years before, she looked at him with alarm and confusion. Then she remembered her plan, the air rifle, and that crazy afternoon. She felt an uncomfortable happiness when she remembered those lost details, as Danilo talked and cracked jokes. She liked his house, the atmosphere, the camaraderie. She stayed for tea with Danilo, his wife, and their son, a dark-skinned, long-haired boy who spoke like an adult. The woman looked at Yasna intensely, then asked what she did to stay so thin.

"I've always been thin," she replied.

"Me, too," said the boy. She bought a lot of marijuana, and Danilo also threw in some seeds.

It'll be a while before the plant flowers. She is watering it now while she listens to the news on the radio. Her father doesn't rape her anymore, he wouldn't be able to. She hasn't forgiven him, she has reached a point where she doesn't believe in forgiveness, or in love, or in happiness, but maybe she believes in death, or at least she waits for it. While she moves the living room furniture around, she thinks about what her life will be when he dies: it's an abstract feeling of freedom, maybe too abstract, and for that reason uncomfortable. She thinks of an ambiguous pain, of a disaster, calm and silent.

She hears her father's complaints coming from the kitchen, his degraded, corrupted voice. Sometimes he shouts at her, berates her, but she ignores him. Other times, especially when he is high, he laughs his labored laughter, utters disjointed phrases. She thinks about the will to live, about her father clinging to life, who knows what for. She brings him another pot cookie, turns on the TV for him, puts his headphones on him. She stays awhile beside him, looking at a magazine. "I didn't believe in God, but only with his help could I overcome the pain," says a famous actor about his wife's death. "It's simple: lots of water," says a model on another page. "Don't let the bullies get to you." "It's her second TV series so far this year." "There are many ways to live." "I didn't know what I was getting mixed up in." "It may take a lot of effort to accomplish everything you need to do."

She hears the garbage truck going by, the men's shouts, the dog barking, the whisper of canned laughter coming from the headphones, she hears her father's breathing and her own breathing, and all those sounds don't alter her feeling of silence—not of peace: of silence. Then she goes to the living room, rolls herself a joint, and smokes it in the darkness.

Part 5

emboldened by solitude, I drove carefully around, fumbling my way for almost two hours, until I found a better place to park it.

I spent my days in a state of inebriation, watching movies in the big bed and sullenly receiving the neighbors' condolences. I was, finally, free. That my freedom so resembled abandonment seemed like a minor detail. I quit school without thinking about it much, since I didn't see myself studying to take the Calculus I test for the third time. I could live on the money my mother sent me, so I forgot about the truck until the night Luis Miguel came to ask me for it. I remember I opened the door apprehensively, but Luis Miguel's friendly manner immediately dispelled my suspicions. After introducing himself and apologizing for the hour, he said that he had heard I had a truck and he wanted to propose I rent it to him. "I can drive it and pay you a weekly fee," he said. I replied that I had little to no interest in the truck, and for me it would be better to sell it. He told me he didn't have any money, that we should at least try the arrangement for a while, and he could take care of finding a buyer later on. He seemed desperate, though later I realized he wasn't, that in his case desperation was more like a habit, a way of being in the world. I invited him in, offered him potato chips and beer, and what happened next was the same as always: we drank so many beers that the next day I woke up next to him, with an aching body and a strong urge to cry. Luis Miguel hugged me cautiously, almost affectionately, and cracked a joke I don't remember, some nonsense that eased my sadness, and I thanked him for it, or tried to, with a look. Then we cooked pasta and improvised a watery sauce, and that day we drank two boxes of wine.

He had promised his wife he wouldn't sleep with men anymore. She didn't care if he went to bed with other women, but she couldn't stand his sleeping with men. By then I was clear on the fact that I didn't like women; I had at first slept with girls my own age, but later it was exclusively men, almost always older ones, though not as old as Luis Miguel, who was forty-four and had two kids and was unemployed.

"You're hired," I told him, and we burst out laughing, already back in bed. Luis Miguel's arms were two or three times thicker than mine. His cock was two inches longer than mine. His skin was darker and softer than mine.

The next month, Luis Miguel invited me to La Calera, and then to Antofagasta, and after that the invitations weren't necessary: for a year and a half we worked together as partners, splitting the earnings. We transported anything: rubble, vegetables, wood, blankets, fireworks, suspicious unmarked boxes. I won't go so far as to say those trips felt short; we had fun, we lightened the journey with jokes and talked about our lives, but little by little the highway would erase the words, and we'd endure the final miles sighing in annoyance. When we got back we would sleep for an entire day and then have sex until we were sated, or until Luis Miguel started feeling guilty, which happened often, regularly. He would interrupt our caresses to jump up and call his wife and tell her he was close to Santiago, and I accepted that comedic routine without complaint because I knew that it wasn't, really, a comedy. "One of my sons is your age," he told me one night, his eyes shot through, not with blood or with rage, exactly; what was in his eyes was a black and bottomless shame that I didn't understand then, don't understand now, and will never understand.

2

"He's a friend of mine," I told Nadia.

Luis Miguel greeted her with embarrassment as he walked past in the nude. He had just woken up, it was ten or eleven in the morning, and Nadia smiled or hinted at a smile: she'd come by to ask for my help moving. "I can't take living with my parents anymore," she told me, and though I didn't ask for specifics, she still started talking with her usual nervous warmth. Soon we set off, all three of us, to get the truck and drive to Nadia's house, where we worked to a soundtrack of my friend's sobs and her mother's wailing. Later, in the truck, Nadia wasn't crying anymore; she laughed enthusiastically, almost giddily. We drove from Maipú to a small apartment on Diagonal Paraguay, where she planned to live with a girl-friend. It was a sixth-floor walk-up but the move was easy, because her things ("my possessions," as she called them) consisted of a mattress, two suitcases, and six boxes of books. On the way back, Luis Miguel asked me about Nadia, and I told him I'd known her for years, ever since we were kids, and that she was my best friend, or had been, at one time, my best friend.

Two weeks later we had to do the trip all over again. We had just gotten back from Valparaíso when Nadia called and begged us to save her from her friend: a crazy woman, she told me, an asshole who thinks I'm her maid. It took me a while to realize that Nadia wasn't going back to her parents' house but was moving into mine. "I talked to your mom about it," she told me, "and she was happy to hear we'd be living together." Contrary to what I expected, Luis Miguel liked the idea.

"We have to find a name," said Nadia that night, while we were doing crossword puzzles. "A trademark, a brand, a *nombre de fantasia*."

"A fantasy name for what?"

"For our moving company," she replied, happy and solemn: "No more long trips, no more highways," she said, and we agreed, and we spent what remained of the night thinking of "fantasy names," until finally Nadia said, beaming: "The best name is Fantasy, Fantasy Movers," and we accepted it, pleased.

The next day, Nadia designed signs and bought overalls for the three of us. Soon we had our first client, a lawyer about to get married who was moving to a big house in Ñuñoa, and from then on we didn't stop: "People around here move a lot, it's like a virus," said Nadia whenever anyone asked how business was going. We painted the truck with some strange images that Luis Miguel thought were awful, and he was right, but we liked the idea of disrupting that uniform landscape of semidetached houses with our outlandish moving truck. We liked our new, quasi-entrepreneurial life, and we spent hours making plans and fixing up the house with the many donations our customers left us. The living room filled up with lamps, wobbly chairs, emptied trunks.

One morning, my mother showed up out of the blue. By that point, nearly three years after my father's death, we hardly ever talked on the phone. She did send me letters, long and affectionate ones written in light handwriting and with an astonishing number of ellipses (*The south . . . is the most beautiful place in the universe . . . Osorno is a quiet city . . . and I've reconnected with . . . my sisters*). It was my birthday, but I certainly wasn't expecting her to visit, much less to open the

front door with her old key and come into her former bedroom to find me asleep in Luis Miguel's arms.

My mother started to cry or moan, and I tried to reassure
her, but she only wailed louder. Eventually, Nadia and a sort
of occasional boyfriend of hers came to see what was happening. The boyfriend took off immediately; Nadia made two
speedy cups of Nescafé and shut herself in her room with my
mother all day. Luis Miguel stayed with me, listened with
me to the sobbing and shouting and the mysterious, silent
ellipsis that came from the room next door.

The two of them only came out as night was falling. My
mother hugged me and shook Luis Miguel's hand, and we ate
the cheese and pastries and drank the cherry brandy that
she'd brought, and she got so drunk that she insisted on singing "Happy Birthday." "It's not every day you have a birthday,"
said my mother before she started to sing and wave her hands.

Luis Miguel hardly ever saw his family by then, but that
day he had to leave at midnight. I slept in Nadia's room, the
two of us sharing a rusty sofa bed a customer had recently
given us. My mother slept in the big bed and took off very
early the next morning. She left a note and a twenty-thousand-
peso bill on the table.

The note said only: Take care of yourselves.

3

We had a lot of work, but we enjoyed it. We even started to
think about buying a second truck, maybe hiring another
person. But the story ended a different way:

Luis Miguel came over, very nervous and holding a bottle
of whiskey. "It's for you," he told us. "You're my friends, we

have to celebrate, you *have* to be happy with my news." I
feared the worst. I wasn't wrong. He said that at the end of
the month he would be moving, with his wife and kids, into
a house of his own in Puente Alto. He said it was far away,
but that it wouldn't be a problem. "We can still work together," he said. I received his words with rage and sadness. I
didn't want to cry, but I cried. Nadia cried too, though it
wasn't really for her to cry about. Luis Miguel raised his
voice, as though jumping ahead in a scene he had perhaps
rehearsed in front of the mirror—he seemed beside himself, but that's all it was, an act: he yelled and pounded the
table with false emphasis. He talked about the future, about
dreams, children, opportunities, about a real world we knew
nothing about. That's what he talked about most, a real world
that the two of us didn't understand. Nadia answered for
both of us: "On October 31, we'll be at your house at nine in
the morning, write down the address and wrap the furniture
carefully. Fantasy Movers will do the move for free, you
motherfucker, now get out of here and start looking for another job."

The days that followed were horrible. Horrible and unnecessary.

The morning of the 31st, we arrived fifteen minutes late.
Luis Miguel lived in an inner apartment of an old building
for low-income residents. One of his sons came to the door;
it was the one who was my age, but he looked older than me.
He looked a lot like his father: the same bushy eyebrows, the
same black eyes, the same dark cast of his cheeks, the large
and beautiful body. The younger son was a very dark-skinned

boy of six or seven who wandered around reading a magazine. Luis Miguel's wife was friendly. The roughness of her features contrasted with her alert eyes; it became difficult not to meet her gaze with a blush. She offered us tea and we declined; she offered us bread and blackberry jam but we excused ourselves. We didn't want to sit at the table with them. It had to be a fast job, we had to look around very little, the bare minimum. But Luis Miguel sought me out with that dry desperation I had occasionally glimpsed, and which now was on full display.

The three of us rode in the truck in utter silence. The wife and kids would come later, so there was time for us to say goodbye. "We won't see each other again," I told him, and he nodded. Nadia hugged him affectionately. I didn't hug him: I left and waited outside for my friend for two or ten interminable minutes. We hadn't talked about it, but Nadia and I knew that we wanted, that in some way we *had* to leave him the truck. It was mad, stupid, a foolish and sentimental waste of money, but we were in agreement. We walked many blocks to catch a bus, and we made it home after an eternal ride, hand in hand.

A couple of weeks ago Nadia started working as a secretary. She goes out very early, leaves me books and cigarettes, and when she comes back we drink long cups of tea. "Maybe you should write this story," she told me this morning, before she left.

Okay, Nadia, I've written it.

Cyclops

First, you have to live, Claudia said, and it was hard not to agree: before you could write, you had to live the stories, the adventures. Back then, I wasn't interested in telling stories. She was, or actually she wasn't, not yet: what she wanted was to live the stories that maybe years or decades later, in an uncertain and tranquil future, she would tell. Claudia was Cortazarian as could be, although her first experience with Cortázar had been, in reality, a disappointment: when she reached chapter 7 of *Hopscotch*, she recognized, in horror, the very text that her boyfriend would often recite to her as his own. As a result, she broke up with him and began a romance with Cortázar that perhaps continues to this day. My friend was not, is not, named Claudia: I'm protecting her identity, just in case, and also that of her ex-boyfriend, who in those days was a teacher's assistant and surely today teaches classes on Cortázar or Lezama Lima or intertextuality at some university in the United States.

At that point, in 1993 or 1994, Claudia was already, no doubt about it, the protagonist of a long, beautiful, and complex novel, worthy of Cortázar or Kerouac or anyone else who might dare to follow her fast, intense life. Other people's lives—our lives—on the other hand, could fit easily onto one page (double-spaced, at that). At eighteen years old, Claudia had already been there and back several times: from one city to another, one country to another, one continent to another, and also, above all, from pain to joy and joy to pain. She filled her notebooks with what I always supposed were stories or sketches for stories or maybe a diary. But the one time she read some of the pieces to me, I discovered, to my astonishment, that she wrote poems. She didn't call them poems, but rather *annotations*. The only real difference between those annotations and the texts that I wrote back then was the level of imposture: we transcribed the same sentences, described the same scenes, but she promptly forgot them or at least claimed to, while I recopied them neatly and wasted hours trying out different titles and structures.

You should write stories, or a novel, I told Claudia that afternoon of cold wind and chilled beer. You've lived through a lot, I added, clumsily. No, she replied, categorically: you've lived more, you've lived much more than me, and then she started to tell my life story as if she were reading my palm, past, present, and future. She exaggerated, as all fiction writers (and all poets) do: random childhood anecdotes became fundamental, every event signified a decisive loss or advancement. I half identified myself in the protagonist, and could partially recognize the decisive secondary characters (she herself was, in the story, a secondary character who took on importance little by little). I wanted to match that novel by improvising Claudia's life story, too: I talked about travel, about her difficult return to Chile, her parents' separation, and I would have kept going, but suddenly Claudia told me to be quiet and went to the bathroom or said she was going to the bathroom, and she didn't come back for ten or twenty minutes. She returned with slow steps, masking, just barely, a fear or shame I hadn't seen in her before. I'm sorry, she said, I don't know if I'd like for someone to write my life story. I'd like to tell it myself, or maybe not have it told at all. We lay in the grass and exchanged apologies as if we were competing in a good manners contest. But, in reality, we were speaking a private language that neither of us knew how to translate, or wanted to.

That was when she told me about chapter 7 of *Hopscotch*. Because I knew that particular TA and I knew he'd been Claudia's boyfriend, the story struck me as even more comic; I pictured him as the cyclops Cortázar spoke of (". . . and then we play cyclops, we look at each other closer each time and our eyes grow, they grow closer, they overlap . . ."). I suppressed my laughter until Claudia let out a guffaw and told me it wasn't true, but we both knew it was. I don't really like Cortázar, I blurted out suddenly, maybe just to change the subject. Why not? I don't know, I just don't really like him, I repeated, and we laughed again, this time for no reason, now free of the stifling seriousness.

It would be easy, now, to refute or confirm those clichés: if you have lived a lot you write novels, if you've only lived a little you write poems. But that wasn't exactly our argument, which wasn't an argument, or at least not the kind where one person wins and the other loses. We wanted, perhaps, to tie, to go on talking until they set the dogs on us and we had to run away, drunk, leaping over the sky-blue fence. But we weren't drunk yet, and the guard couldn't care less whether we left or went right on talking all night long.

Story of
a Sheet

1. It was before my dad set the house on fire. Fifteen or twenty days before.

2. There was a closet full of sheets, almost all of them white with red stitching, Italian red. Plus a light blue set that was mine, patterned with blue letters or treble clefs.

3. My mother, her back to me, in front of a white sheet; fifteen or twenty days ago, before, facing a white sheet. She wasn't crying. She was standing there, simply, waiting for the sheet to dry.

4. It was a lightless day. She turned around and came over to the window and looked at me, she imitated my face looking at her, even tried to smile. But then she didn't come inside. She went back to her spot in front of the sheet.

5. A sheet drying in the wind on a windless day. A canvas, a kind of scene. The scene continues until the audience understands that there will be no second act.

6. I'm the one who starts the round of applause. I used to work doing voice-overs, but I was fired. Now I'm the guy who starts the applause.

7. My job is to hit things off, to break into applause, to give a big hand. My job is to close my hands, bring them forcibly together, with force. My job is to seek out silences and fill them.

8. I'll clap you—in the face! they said to me sometimes, but as a joke.

9. Don't let the door hit you on the way out, they told me, but as a joke.

10. Go see if it's raining on the corner.

11. Long before, years before, my father had to rush home for an emergency; his wife was about to give birth to me.

12. But it's a clean image, new and false. As it should be. The children playact being wounded among the climbing vines.

13. Once upon a time there was a white sheet drying in the sun. But it was a sunless day. It's a very long story.

14. There is no second sheet. The sheet lengthens out, unfolds, but there is no other sheet inside.

15. Once upon a time there was a sheet around a white body.

16. Once upon a time there was a sheet that stained.

17. It seems they wrapped someone up. I don't remember well, I was a little out of it.

18. "Don't pose," they tell him, but it's hard not to pose. Even in dreams. Sometimes he fakes nightmares. Wakes up with a shout, a shout of his own. And though he knows there was no call for shouting, he accepts a tired embrace from someone, from nobody, and keeps quiet.

19. Don't dream, don't pose, gradually fall asleep. That's how it's said, gradually.

20. Once upon a time there was a sheet drying gradually.

21. Days before my dad set the house on fire, there was a sheet drying gradually.

22. I'm not going to open the window. Stop asking. It doesn't open.

23. In love or in error, they sleep together.

24. The body grows or contracts during a night of sleep. The face loses and finds its features with the touch of the pillow.

25. Careful, your body could split in two.

26. Turn off the color bars and go back to sleep.

27. In the dream the cars went right past.

28. The smoke arrives before the voices.

29. The ghosts left the table set for us.

30. Once upon a time there was a shape and a sheet.

West Cemetery

Y ou don't have the right to do that," the woman said to
him. Her tone was rather sweet, as though in feigned
reproach.

"I'm sorry," he replied, automatically.

He was in Amherst, Massachusetts, at the West Cemetery, reading letters that had been left by visitors to Emily
Dickinson's grave. They weren't letters, exactly, but little slips
of paper quickly dashed off in homage. *You are not nobody to
me!!!* one of the messages said, and there were actually more
like ten exclamation points, which struck him as shrill, depressingly eager.

"I think the people who wrote those messages would want
someone to read them," he said, but his words sounded guilty
to him, as often happened when he spoke English: he couldn't
strike the right tone, didn't have his own style; he spoke with
borrowed phrases, as though imitating someone, anyone else.

"You look like a jealous man looking through his wife's
things," she said.

He didn't answer, but looked at her round face, her wild,
nearly blond hair, her black eyes where he thought he glimpsed
the extra shine of contact lenses, though of course he couldn't
be sure she was wearing contacts.

"I'm from here," the woman said.

"I'm not," he replied, as if that were necessary to clarify.

He had woken up at five in the morning, fixated on the idea of making the trip out to Amherst. It wasn't totally a whim; it was more of a retroactive decision, almost like righting a past wrong. He'd wanted to go to Amherst for years, ever since his first trip to New York City, when his English was, so to speak, Dickinsonian. Really, his English back then was nearly nonexistent; it mostly came from music and TV, but also from his attempts to decipher Emily Dickinson's poems, which he had read for the first time at the age of twenty in a translation published in Spain that he hadn't liked at all, but since the edition was bilingual he had adapted it a little, combining his scant knowledge of English with a little intuition. He had translated the Spanish Spanish into Chilean Spanish, somewhat like a student copying answers on a test.

It was a freezing cold day in early December, and a snowstorm was imminent. Lately, he'd had the feeling that everyone in New York talked exclusively about the weather, like in the Paul Simon song: "I can gather all the news I need on the weather report." He'd been reading *The Gorgeous Nothings*, the lovely facsimile edition of Dickinson's "envelope poems," but he didn't want to go to Amherst lugging such a heavy tome. He lived in a Crown Heights apartment that was full of books, and he thought there must be another collection of Emily Dickinson's poetry somewhere on the shelves, but he only found—classified under E for Emily and not D for Dickinson—*My Emily Dickinson*, Susan Howe's beautiful and intense critical work.

The feeling that he was setting off on an urgent journey stayed with him from the moment he left the apartment until he boarded the half-empty Peter Pan bus at Port Authority. He sat in the last seat remembering *Kensington Gardens*, Rodrigo Fresán's novel about J. M. Barrie. Fifteen minutes after leaving the station, he heard the shy tapping of snow on the roof. He looked out the window wondering if he would ever get used to the snow, if it would ever stop seeming wonderful, if someday he would look out the window and see the streets covered in white and think: Shit, it's snowing.

It was also snowing in Hartford, where the bus stopped for five minutes, and in Springfield, where he changed buses and managed to smoke a quick cigarette huddled in the smoking area, but it wasn't snowing in Amherst. When he got off the bus he felt the same freezing wind hit his face that he'd felt when he left the apartment, and he was happy at the childish thought that he had beaten the snow there, that it was on the way, running a little late, from New York.

He wandered aimlessly, not wanting to check the map on his phone, but Amherst was so small that five minutes later he was in the West Cemetery. Atop Dickinson's grave, in addition to the letters, there was a graphite pencil, a dried carnation, a bouquet of other flowers in the process of drying out—roses, carnations—a Little Mermaid doll, a figurine of a rat eating something, a watch stopped at noon or midnight, a button depicting a smiling boy and a goose beneath the words *Pssst, Happy Founder's Day, Mary Lyon!*, a safety pin, a few coins, and some rocks, among them two that were almost identical and almost round.

"I smoked my first cigarette here," the woman said suddenly, as if he'd asked (as if before, somewhere else, he had asked her that question).

"The first time you came?" he asked.

"No, I came here all the time when I was a kid. Like I told you, I'm from here. I've lived my whole life a five-minute walk from here." She started to look at the letters, too, and she picked up the coins, seemed to count them, and organized them into stacks of nickels, pennies, and dimes.

He offered her a cigarette, but she declined.

"And did you come to the cemetery to play back when you were a kid?"

"I came to leave pennies for Emily, in case she needed money in heaven." She counted the coins again, though it seemed more like she was looking at the lines on her own hands with something like curiosity. "Then I felt guilty, and I came back to leave more coins."

"Guilty for what?"

"I thought the other dead people might need money, too."

He imagined her as a child running among the graves and dropping pennies. Her face wasn't that of a child; it was the kind of young face that is easy to project into the future but not into the past.

"Read me a poem," she said, pointing to the book he was holding.

Instead, he handed her the book, and she flipped through it, lingering on the poems that Susan Howe cited.

"You didn't have a book of hers, of Emily's?" she asked.

He shook his head. She kept paging through the book for a couple more minutes. This is the moment when I should ask what her name is, he thought. He didn't ask.

"Well, it looks good anyway," she said.

"It *is* good."

"Where are you from?"

"I'm from Chile," he said.

"Chile," she repeated, with the expression of someone trying to call up a hazy memory. "I'll buy this book from you,"
she said. "All these coins add up to a little over a dollar."

"Okay," he replied.

She handed him the coins and left with the book, practically running. He stayed beside the grave and smoked a cigarette. It started to snow, and he saw the flakes falling onto the
letters. He tried to cover them with the rocks.

The rest of the day he behaved like a tourist. He visited the
museum-house, bought postcards, and took pictures for other
tourists, who in turn took pictures of him while he thought
confusedly about clarity and isolation and beauty. He returned to New York in speedy, half-empty buses. The next
day he got another copy of Susan Howe's book, a more recent
edition, to replace the one from the shelf: it was like completing an old building with a new brick.

Months passed; he returned to Chile and soon got used to
the absence of snow. One day, in the pocket of his backpack,
he found the coins the woman had given him, and tossed
them into the container of change he kept to give as tips.
Since that day, almost a year has passed. A couple of hours
ago he ordered a pizza, and when it arrived, he grabbed a
handful of coins to tip the delivery boy, who was in fact an
old man, skinny and gray with a bitter expression. Lately the
delivery people tend to be old, and yet I'm always surprised,

he mused. He usually thinks of pizza delivery people as delivery boys. Maybe they grow old doing that, delivering pizzas, he thought.

He was about to bite into the first slice when a rock hit the window. He went outside. The crack was faint, and he didn't think he would need to replace the glass, at least not right away. Among the plants in the garden he found a medium-size stone and twelve cents: two nickels and two pennies. He pictured the delivery man looking at the tip, furious at those small and useless coins. He apologized in his head, explaining that he'd grabbed several coins, as always, maybe ten of them, without thinking that those foreign cents might sneak into his fist. He imagined the delivery man apologizing too, in turn, for stoning his window. He imagined that the conversation went on, that the pizza grew cold but they stood and smoked a cigarette together while the delivery man told his life story, and he told the delivery man about Amherst and the snow and Emily Dickinson and that other woman whose name he hadn't asked.

Penultimate Activities

1

In a Word document, using a maximum of five thousand characters including spaces, describe, in the greatest possible detail, the house where you live. Observe the walls especially. Note the cracks, the stains, the nail marks and holes. Think, for example, of how many times those walls have been painted. Imagine the brushes, the gallons of paint, the rollers. Think of the people who painted those walls. Call up their faces, invent them.

Next, consider the leaks, the imperfections in the floors, the carpets (if there are carpets), the drawers that don't close all the way, the kitchen utensils, the condition of handles and outlets, the shape and quality of the mirrors (if there are mirrors): pay special attention to what the mirrors reflect when no one is looking, and a suspicion of uselessness settles over them.

2

Organize any books in the house according to size, not from largest to smallest, but rather forming waves or pyramids. Do not think, please, about the possibility of reading them—<u>that is not the purpose of this activity</u>. Nor should you pay any mind to the titles or the authors: confront the books as if they were mere imperfect bricks. Then set them on fire and watch the flames from a prudent distance. Let the blaze grow, but try not to let it get out of control. Inhale a little smoke, close your eyes every once in a while, ideally for no longer than ten seconds. Think of this: every fire, slight or brief as it may be, is a spectacle. Think of the clouds when the trees burn. Then, try to extinguish the fire. Do it calmly and with care, elegantly if possible. Finally, look up at the sky, where God or one of his epigones should be, and give thanks.

If you were able to control the fire, if by this point you are not dead or aboard an ambulance, if you managed—with or without faith—to give thanks to God or one of his epigones, you will see some books that are blackened and unrecognizable, and others that are half burnt, or almost completely destroyed but still recognizable, even legible, and also a group of almost intact books that are maybe a little wet or smudged, but salvageable. Gather up the ruined books, place them in suitcases you don't use much or in heavy-duty garbage bags, large or extra large; walk to the nearest river, toss the baggage into the current, look at the sky and give thanks, but this time with no real ceremony, without emphasis, with true familiarity toward God or his epigones or toward the entity that fulfills or should fulfill a certain transcendent function.

If there is no reasonably close river, leave the bags in the place where, if you lived in a different city, in a city you had designed, whether well or badly, there would be a river. Stand and stare at the current, concentrate on the current until you feel as if you were moving forward.

Back at home, read the books that survived the fire, and (a) draw your conclusions, but don't belabor your theories: simply postulate some ideas, abstruse as they may be, about the meaning of the fact—fair or unfair, but always arbitrary— that it was these and not other books that were saved from the fire, and (b) think, but without an ounce of dramatics or self-pity, about whether these books could somehow save you.

3

Type out your impressions about activity number 2 in a Word file, 12 point Perpetua font, double-spaced, using a minimum of twenty thousand characters, including spaces.

4

Repeat activity number 2 until there are no legible or recognizable books in your house. Always give thanks, though you don't need to look at the sky, just raise your eyebrows. Every time, concentrate on the river, on the current (until you feel you're moving forward).

Then, when there are no more books, open a new document. Now write with no limitations on length, using the font that most resembles your own handwriting, or your handwriting as you remember it. Now go ahead and write about your life: about your childhood, about love, about fear.

And about the opposite of fear, the opposite of love, the opposite of childhood. And about hunger, coughing, all of it. Think back, don't idealize, but neither should you avoid idealization. If you talk about people who were once close but who now seem remote, do not theorize about distance; try to understand that old nearness. Don't avoid sentimentalism or gerunds.

Then, select all the text, copy and paste it into another file, and erase the characters you sincerely feel should never have been born, because they hurt you or the people you love.

5

Combine all the files into one, in whatever order you prefer. The page setting should be letter-size, single spaced and with your choice of font, though 12 point Perpetua is recommended. Number the pages in the lower right-hand corner, choose a title, sign it with your name or a pseudonym or the name you think should have been yours, the name you would have liked to have. Only then, for the first time, should you print it all out and bind it. You have written a book, and this time you don't have to thank anyone for it. You have written a book, but don't publish it. If you want, write others and publish them, but don't ever publish this one.

CHILEAN POET
A Novel

An aspiring poet reunites with his first love and, together with her young son, forms a stepfamily. Though the arrangement doesn't last, the boy inherits his ex-stepfather's love of poetry. At eighteen, he encourages an American journalist to write about the endearingly dysfunctional world of Chilean poets in this tender, insightful novel about family in all its forms.

BONSAI
A Novel

Bonsai, Alejandro Zambra's landmark first novel, now in a brilliant new translation, tells the story of two Chilean university students who, seeking truth in great literature, find each other instead. As they fall together and drift apart over the course of young adulthood, Zambra spins an emotionally engrossing, formally inventive tale of love, art, and memory.

THE PRIVATE LIVES OF TREES
A Novel

Verónica is late, and Julián becomes convinced she won't return. To pass the time, he improvises a story about trees to coax his stepdaughter, Daniela, to sleep. As the night stretches on, Julián finds himself caught up in the slipstream of the story of his life. What combination of desire and coincidence led them here, to this very night?

PENGUIN BOOKS